LOVE IN A SNAPSHOT

CHRISTMAS AT THE FARM

BRITNEY M. MILLS

CRYSTAL CANYON PUBLISHING

CHAPTER 1

shley Morgan glanced at the screen of her phone and groaned as she saw Quincy's name for the fifth time in the last hour. Once the call went to voicemail, the screen showed that there were at least ten text messages from her cousin, all of which Ashley ignored. She'd been so blind, so naïve to think her life was a big fairytale, that she was finally getting her happily ever after.

The memory of Jason's face as he told her he could no longer marry her was burned into her brain, making it difficult to keep the tears from forming. And what was worse was the fact that his attentions had switched to Quincy Morgan, Ashley's closest female cousin and coworker.

Everything seemed to have imploded in the last twenty-four hours, and she wasn't sure how she was going to pick up the pieces of her life. Of course, since she was a travel blogger and social media influencer, the easiest thing was to book a flight and head out, hoping that the events from yesterday would become a distant memory sooner rather than later. And here she sat, in the Houston airport, waiting for her flight to begin boarding.

The phone rang again, and the irritation flared up. Setting her jaw, Ashley swiped to answer the call. "What?" Her tone was surprisingly devoid of emotion, given the circumstances.

"Ashley, please, don't hang up. Just let me explain. We didn't mean for things to happen like this." Quincy kept talking, and Ashley shook her head. Wasn't that the line that every cheater had used on every victim in the history of the world?

"You were gone for a long time, and Jason helped take care of me after my knee surgeries. We just started falling for each other. Just know I did everything I could to fight it; I really did. I know how much he means to you, and if you're not going to talk to me, I'll break up with him."

Oh good. The future of her cousin's love life was now in Ashley's hands.

She paused for several seconds, trying to decide which road to travel. It would be easy to be cruel and vindictive, to give some of the bitterness she felt to her cousin. But was that the right thing? Her grandmother's voice seemed to tug at the back of her mind, saying she'd regret severing this friendship.

"What did you expect? Quincy, I can't talk about this right now. I'm still in shock about the whole thing. I never would've believed you could betray me like that. You've been my best friend since we were in diapers. I—I, well, I think I just need some time to sort things through." Ashley heard a breath of relief on the other line, not helping to quench the fire of her temper simmering. "Don't contact me for a while."

She clicked the end button, brushing away a tear that escaped down the side of her face. Probably not the words Grandma Morgan would have liked, but at least she'd been grown up enough to not hang up on her former best friend.

She and Quincy had been inseparable since grade school, and when Ashley had posed the idea of traveling the world after high school graduation, they'd found a way to make it work. Sometimes, they'd stay in places for several months to save up money for the next adventure, taking on odd jobs here and there. And then one day, one of the major national news stations had highlighted their blog, and it seemed like life changed overnight. They were now getting paid to fly to exotic destinations and promote certain brands.

But how could she continue to work with her cousin after all this? What was a twenty-seven-year-old woman supposed to do with only a high school diploma?

She'd held countless jobs from waitress to janitor to assistant over the years. There was even one time when she'd been a farmhand in a small Nebraska town. She had a lot more experience in a wide range of jobs but none that she loved as much as the overall writing, taking pictures, and talking about travel.

"Now boarding, Flight 544 for Jackson, Wyoming," sounded over the intercom.

Ashley stood, grateful for the distraction from her desperate thinking. She'd asked the ticket agent downstairs for the next departing flight and was surprised to find the destination was the small tourist town that had always been on her list of places to visit. It was now or never, and maybe dropping off the grid for a few days would do her some good.

She scanned her phone under the sensor and waited for the ding that allowed her to board. A window seat and some sleep were all she wanted at that moment. She'd have to face all this at some point, but not now.

CHAPTER 2

$\mathcal{P}$reston Burke attached the milking machine to several of the cows he'd herded into the milking pen, trying to be grateful they hadn't put up much fuss tonight. It could have been worse. He could've had to hand milk each cow on the farm at least twice a day. The thought made him thankful that wasn't the case.

It was the end of October, and he was already itching to get away from the farm where he'd spent the last few years, day in and day out, except for the occasional vacation to a far-off beach. If only he hadn't been born first, then maybe he'd still be on the rodeo circuit.

Shaking his head, he knew that wasn't the case. His father's stroke a few years ago had changed all that, making things in Preston's life difficult for a while.

He'd just gotten used to being back in Coldwater Creek and working on the farm when his younger sister, Lauren, had married his best friend Walker last spring. And then Easton's marriage to the new English teacher at the high school had thrown him. The only real relationship he'd been in was a short stint with Walker's younger sister, Kassidy, the previous winter. But she'd needed to get out more, see the world. Being stuck with a dairy farmer wasn't going to help fulfill those dreams.

He was a twenty-nine-year-old male with no real prospects for a future. It was the same drudgery every day, but if he kept dwelling on that, he'd go insane.

A few minutes later, the machine beeped at him, and he began unhooking the machine from the cow udders, making sounds and slapping their behinds to get them back out the door and ready for the next row of cows.

"Don't look so excited," came a voice from behind him. He turned to find one of his younger brothers with his arms folded against his chest, leaning on the door frame to the small building.

"You look just as happy to be working out here, Seth." Preston gave him a playful jab on the shoulder. His brother was only seventeen but would probably pass Preston in height, although his build was much leaner like their mother's side of the family.

"I cleaned out the hen house. Do you need anything else? Or can I head into town with some of my friends?" Seth's face looked hopeful, his eyes wide and pleading for this break.

Preston chuckled. "I'm not the one to ask about that. I think I just saw Dad walk inside. Go ask him."

Seth didn't take long to react to that, taking long strides and making it into the house in less than a minute.

That was the hard part about taking over the daily jobs of the dairy farm. Their father was there mentally, but his physical capabilities were limited. He would always send the three boys out to ask Preston what chores they needed to get done before they could do things with friends, but Preston felt odd to have that much power when their father was still around. A weird cycle that he wished could somehow end.

An hour later, the milking was all done, the machinery cleaned to his father's specifications, and he was ready for a shower. He checked his phone as he walked inside, hoping to find a text message with something to do on this Friday night. There had been a lot to do before, well, before all of his friends had gotten married and settled down. Now he just felt like the third wheel anytime they invited him places.

Lauren had even offered to set him up for a double date with them, but the options were slim in Coldwater Creek. Not that he was overly picky, but he'd known most of the women in the valley since he was in grade school, and if there was ever going to be a spark, it would have happened by now.

After a quick shower, he pulled on a plaid button-up shirt and grabbed his favorite faded baseball cap.

"Where are you off to?" his father's voice trailed him.

Turning, Preston smiled. "I'm not sure yet, Dad. I think I'll just go for a drive."

"You can always come watch the game with me when you get back. It's just now starting." His father was an avid baseball fan and never missed a game when one of his favorite teams was playing. And now that it was the post-season, it seemed like every night had "the game" on.

"Sounds good. Do you need me to pick up anything in town?"

A mischievous grin caused Preston to chuckle. "Get me some more pop. I think I just drank the last one."

Shaking his head, Preston chuckled. "Mom would be all over you for that. Who knows? Maybe she's looking down right now and giving you a hard time."

His father's face sobered, and Preston wished he could take back the words. There hadn't been a love quite like the one between his parents. The way they'd beamed when the other walked into the room was something to be admired, especially after twenty-four years of marriage. If only she'd lived a little longer, maybe she'd be able to tell Preston what to do about his life and how to get out of the funk he now found himself in.

Preston gave him a tight smile. "Right. I'll get you some root beer. Text me if you think of anything else." He turned and hurried out the door, not wanting to spark any more sadness for his father.

The whole Burke family missed their matriarch and the light she'd brought to so many just from her bubbly personality. But no one missed her more than her husband, who thought about her almost constantly throughout the day and oftentimes wandered the halls of the old farmhouse at night as if he could talk to her.

Preston hopped into his newer model Chevy truck, the last glimmer of his life from the rodeo. As he drove into town, he tried to sing along with the radio, hoping to keep his thoughts from the sadness and loneliness beginning to creep in. He needed to find a solution and fast. With winter coming on, there wouldn't be much chance for him to get away from the farm, which would only make things harder.

CHAPTER 3

After spending a few days wandering through Jackson, Ashley rented a car and decided to go for a drive. Many of the locals had talked about the beauty surrounding Jackson Hole, and she couldn't wait to see what else there was around this beautiful country.

She wound her way through the canyon and down into Alpine, finding a small town with a few amenities. With plenty of gas in the tank, she continued down the two-lane road, admiring the beauty of the surrounding pines and the wide valley. She'd passed a sign at one point that said Coldwater Creek Valley, and the name stuck with her.

The beauty of the river snaking its way through the fields made her stop a few times to take pictures, the blog post already tumbling through her brain for her readers. But she couldn't post it, at least not yet. Quincy had called once that morning, but Ashley had turned her phone off, not ready for the emotional rollercoaster that would come if Quincy didn't respect her need for a bit of privacy.

She drove into the town of Afton, pulling into the grocery store parking lot to grab a drink and a few snacks for the drive back. It was already getting dark, and she hadn't clocked how long it had taken for her to drive this far. She just hoped she'd be able to find her way back to Jackson.

Walking into the grocery store, she surveyed the signs above the aisles, looking for the right one to find her cheddar crackers and peanuts. After grabbing them, she headed over to the coolers, looking for something to quench her thirst.

She moved forward to grab one of the large bottles of whole chocolate milk when another hand touched hers and the bottle at the same time. Ashley jumped back and looked up, her laugh coming out a bit nervous.

"Sorry, go ahead." She pointed for the tall, handsome man to get his drink.

"No, after you." He pointed at the same time.

Ashley chuckled, the sound not as forced this time. "No, really. Go ahead. I'm not in a hurry."

The guy reached forward and grabbed one bottle of milk and then another, handing one of them to Ashley. "Here you go." He paused like he was trying to figure out what to say next, and it was then that Ashley saw the beautiful blue of his eyes. "Not many people I know like to drink this kind of chocolate milk." He looked down and gestured with the bottle.

"This is true. My mom always gave me a hard time for liking something with 'so much fat,' but I love it. The other kinds just taste watered down." Ashley giggled a bit, feeling like a dork for admitting so much to a stranger. A handsome stranger, that is.

He nodded. "Well, it's good to know my mom wasn't the only one to say stuff like that. Enjoy your milk." He smiled at her, the expression causing something inside Ashley to ease up, and for the first time since she'd found out her fiancé was in love with her cousin and best friend, she couldn't help but smile. As he walked away, she watched him go, seeing how built he was in the upper body. Her eyes trailed down to his jeans, and she had to hold back a whistle at the way they made his backside look.

Shaking her head, she turned back to the cooler, reminding herself she did not need to go falling in love with someone on a rebound. She would swear off boys for a while and see how her life turned out.

As she walked toward the register, she saw the man checking out with a large selection of root beer and his chocolate milk. She wished she could get a good view of his face again, but he took the receipt from the cashier and walked out the door before she made it to the check stand.

Why did she care? It wasn't like she was going to be staying in this small town for longer than a few minutes.

"Did you find everything you need?" the cashier asked her with a smile. That brought Ashley back to the present, and she nodded, returning the smile.

"Yes, thank you." She watched as the woman scanned her snacks and waited for the end total. "Is there only one route to Jackson from here?"

The woman looked up and frowned like she was concentrating. "The most direct road is up through Alpine and then through the canyon. But I haven't really tried another way."

"That's what I thought. Is it about an hour from here?"

"Maybe just a bit more. I would travel slowly on those roads at night. It might be a good idea just to rent a room at one of the places to stay around here and head out tomorrow if you have the time. There's a new lodge down the road. Driving to Jackson this late at night can get a bit dicey." The woman finished scanning the snacks and hit a button on the keyboard. "That'll be $32.27, please."

Ashley inserted her credit card into the machine and waited for the instructions to remove it. The woman handed her the receipt, and Ashley picked up the bags and took them with her out the door and into the chilly night. The temperature was a lot different than Texas had been, and she'd only brought a light jacket with her, thinking it was still fall and she would be able to enjoy the colors without having to worry about the chill.

The woman's words rang in her ears, and something about it made her want to stay in this little valley at least until sunlight in the morning. She'd brought along her carry-on, so at least she had a few things for the night. She'd take the safe route for once and then head back to Jackson in the morning.

CHAPTER 4

$\mathcal{P}$reston sat in his truck for a few minutes, enjoying his chocolate milk and replaying the scene with the girl next to the drink cooler. She was attractive, and he'd never met another girl who had the same taste in milk. It was a strange thing to have in common, but he'd loved her laugh and the smile she'd shone when he'd handed her the bottle of milk.

Taking one last swig, he turned on his truck and was about to leave, when he saw her walking out of the store. Curious as to who she was, he waited for her to get into a small compact car with the license plates from California.

"No chance there, Preston," he said out loud to himself. That usually meant she was a tourist or someone passing through, and he knew better than to get attached to someone from out of town. Chances were they'd find the small town a bit too stifling after a while and move on, probably to the busy town of Jackson, north of Coldwater Creek.

He pulled out and drove down the road, doing his best to go through the schedule for the week. Other than the daily milkings, there were a few things he needed to get done around the farm. The weather was so unpredictable that he wasn't sure when it would start snowing, and it was easier to have things all put together before that first frost. Last year it had snowed in early November and then again with the blizzard on Thanksgiving. But from what he'd heard, winter was coming earlier this year.

No matter how hard he tried to concentrate, the woman's face from the store kept popping into his mind, causing him to wonder what it was about her. Maybe the mystery of who she was and what she was doing in the only grocery store in town on a dark night was what had him curious. Or maybe it was the fact that he already knew all the single women his age in town and so someone new made things interesting.

Either way, he just needed to get back into the mentality that he'd be getting up in the morning in the house he'd grown up in and heading out to milk the cows at five in the morning, just like he'd done all his life. A strange girl wasn't bound to change much about that, and he'd probably never see her again anyway.

He parked the truck in the driveway and hauled his dad's twenty-four-pack of pop into the washroom where he kept it on the cabinet by the washer and dryer. Preston grinned at the thought of his mother scolding them all for drinking anything but the milk they produced on the farm and the cool, crisp water of the valley. But every once in a while, it was worth a change to have something different.

Walking into the living room, he found his father snoring in his favorite recliner, the game turned up way louder than a normal human should need it to be. Preston grabbed the remote and turned it down.

As he turned toward his father, a feeling of gratitude and guilt overwhelmed him. The man sitting before him had worked tirelessly his whole life to make sure his kids had a life they wanted. Preston felt bad that he'd been annoyed with the farm for so many years, but the thought of the rodeo, at least the part where he was traveling the country and seeing and meeting new people, was the hardest thing about their situation. His father would do anything for him. It wasn't his fault that he'd had a stroke and couldn't work all the machinery anymore.

That and losing Preston's mother had upturned the Burke family's world in the last few years, and even though his father looked serene in sleep, Preston could see the worry that plagued him. Having to raise several kids on his own and with limited capabilities had been a challenge, but he'd done it so far. The younger three kids, Adam, Tyler, and Seth, were all good, hard-working kids who helped out around the farm as much as possible. But they weren't stuck with it as a future. The thought caused a bitter taste to invade Preston's mouth once again.

Adam had been working as a big-engine mechanic since he'd graduated from trade school the year before. Tyler graduated last May and was working at the gas station a couple miles from the farm, trying to figure out what to do with his life. Seth still had two years left of high school, giving him the most freedom of them all even though he spent most of his time studying for his advanced classes and helping around the home.

Preston plopped onto the couch next to the recliner, leaning forward with his head in his hands. His eyes saw the baseball game playing out on the television, but his brain was trying to stay away from thinking about how unfair everything in his life was. Would he be living here the rest of his life? Alone?

The thought chilled him, and he knew he needed to distract himself. Standing again, he tapped his father on the shoulder. "Dad, Dad. It's time to head to bed."

His father woke up, a small smile on his face. "What time is it?"

Preston glanced up at the big grandfather clock standing next to the wall. "Almost nine thirty. Let's get you ready for the night."

After sitting up the recliner, his father reached out for his hands, and Preston hauled him up. As comfortable as the chair was, it made it hard for his old man to get out of it. He was still partially paralyzed on his right side, making it difficult to get out completely on his own.

Preston moved down the hall and waited for his father to catch up before moving in and grabbing the pajamas he'd worn the night before. It had been a while since he'd helped his father get ready for bed, as Sam or Tyler usually did it when they were home.

His father sat on the bed, and Preston squatted down to pull off the wool socks he liked to wear.

"Are you happy, son?" The question threw Preston off guard and onto his heels. He balanced himself with one hand on the ground.

"Sure, I'm happy, Dad. Why wouldn't I be?" He made sure to avoid eye contact, knowing his father would be able to tell what he'd been thinking earlier.

There was another moment's pause before his father said, "I know being a dairy farmer was never your dream. And I'm sorry things had to happen like they did, with us losing your mother and then the stroke. I just want you to know how much I appreciate your help in keeping this family going." His voice broke, causing tears to spring to Preston's eyes with the emotion. "There are days when I wish I could just move like I did before, that I had all the same capabilities so you wouldn't have to sacrifice so much."

Preston continued removing the socks with his head down. "Dad, it's fine. I don't want to see this family suffer any more than we've already done. It's worth the time to make sure the boys are taken care of, that they have a roof over their heads and food on the table."

A large hand rested on Preston's shoulder, and the weight of it caused Preston to take a sharp breath. He didn't need to show his dad his true feelings from moments before. What he'd said was true; there was no way he would let his family suffer when there was something he could do about it. Maybe if there were more opportunities to escape on a vacation, he wouldn't feel so trapped and disheartened by the work.

"I appreciate that, son. I just hope we'll find a way out of it soon enough. I know you'd do anything to have wings to fly and get out of this small town. I promise I'll do everything I can to make sure it isn't a life-long curse for you." He paused a moment, and when he spoke again, he said, "No man should have to do something he hates for the rest of his life."

Preston focused on the task at hand, pulling up the pajama pants and helping his father with the top, gently guiding the arm through. As much as his spirits lifted at the thought of being free of cows, just about the only way to do that was if they sold the farm to someone or if one of his brothers decided they wanted to take over the farm. At twenty-three, nineteen, and seventeen, that would be years yet.

"There you go, Dad. Let's get your teeth brushed, and then you can get to bed."

"I may have some struggles, but I can still brush my teeth on my own." He smiled, and Preston raised his hands in surrender.

"Sounds good. I'm going to go outside and make sure everything's good for the night. Let me know if you need anything when I come back in." Preston left the room, walking back out into the cool night air.

He took a seat on the back porch, scrubbing his face with his hands. He needed to get out of this funk, to go back to putting his head down and working through the problems he faced. Desperation would get him nowhere, and he still had a long life ahead of him.

He'd find a way to make the life he wanted while living at the farm. He just needed to find an opportunity to do so.

CHAPTER 5

Ashley woke up more rested than she'd felt in quite a few days. The lodge where she'd stopped was cozy, and it seemed as though each of the rooms had a certain nature theme. This one had wolf décor throughout, from the light fixture to the bedsheets. She'd laughed as she'd settled in. She hadn't stayed in a place like this too often. Most of the adventures she'd taken with Quincy had been next to a beach, enjoying the sand as the large waves rolled in.

She packed up her things and walked down the stairs, ready to head back to Jackson. She took her key to the gal behind the desk and thanked her for the room.

As she walked out to her rental car, a woman was getting out of the car next to it. She smiled at Ashley and asked, "Did you enjoy your stay?"

"I did, thank you."

"Great! We'd love to have you again. Did you get breakfast?"

Ashley bit her bottom lip, trying to decide how to answer. She wasn't used to people asking her those kinds of questions, and she debated whether to jump in the car and take off. "No, I'm not really a breakfast kind of person, and I've got to get going."

"No worries. I just wanted to make sure you knew there was a complimentary breakfast if you needed it. I'm Lauren McBride, the hotel manager. My husband, Walker, built this place." She walked over and stuck out her hand for Ashley to shake.

"Nice to meet you. I'm Ashley Morgan."

The woman's eyes went wide. "Are you serious? Like the Ashley Morgan from The Travel Diaries blog?"

It took Ashley's brain a few moments to form a coherent sentence, surprised that someone in this small town knew of her work. "Yeeesss," she said hesitantly.

"Oh my goodness! This is amazing. I've been following your blog and your Quickstagram for the past year, and I have to say, you and your cousin do an amazing job. I'm hoping to get my husband to take a few trips this year. We're coming up on a year of this lodge being opened, and I'm slowly working on getting him to hire people so we can take some time to travel."

"There are some great places to visit, but I have to say, Coldwater Creek is a beautiful place." Ashley looked around at the bits of color on the hillsides.

Lauren grinned. "Yes, it is. I can't complain about that, and I'm glad I live here. It's just nice to get out every once in a while to see all the fun and then appreciate where you live."

"You're very right about that. Well, if you need any suggestions on where to go, just let me know. I have a few options for you." Ashley smiled and thought about the woman's words. "What would you need, help-wise, to go on a vacation for a little bit?"

Lauren's eyebrows narrowed. "That's a good question. We've already found a chef to relieve my husband of that duty, so I guess someone to manage the property while we're gone."

Ashley bit her lip, wondering if she should be offering her services after so long of not doing so. But what did she have to lose? She could stay in this place a little longer and hopefully get past some of the things she'd been stewing over the last few days.

"If you and your husband are willing, I've spent plenty of time in hotels and have also worked in several over the years. Nothing major, but I'm sure with a bit of training from you that I could handle it for a couple of weeks while you take some time to yourselves." Even as the words were pouring out of her mouth, Ashley wondered if she was doing the right thing. She was a stranger in this place. Why did she feel like she needed to stay?

"Are you serious? I would absolutely love that. Here, let me give you a card, and you can call me later today."

Ashley took the card and nodded. "Any chance you want to take a spontaneous trip right away? I'm actually in a great spot to do it. I just need to retrieve the rest of my stuff from my hotel in Jackson, and I can be here later today. Just let me know."

"Are you not working on a project for your blog right now?"

A lump formed in Ashley's throat as she shook her head. "We're taking a, um, much-needed vacation from the blog for a bit. This will be just the thing to help me get back to doing what I love."

Her words struck a chord within her as she realized she needed a break from her work, and from Quincy and Jason. Going back to the thrill of starting a new job, even if it only lasted for a few weeks or months, had always been something Ashley loved when she and Quincy had first started the blog. And that same thrill had gone through her just then.

Lauren nodded. "Great. Well, I'll let you go, and thank you again. You don't know how excited I am about this."

Ashley waved and got into the car, pulling out of the Silver Brook Lodge parking lot and back onto the main highway that would take her back to Jackson. She was ready for an adventure, and it seemed like she'd stumbled upon the perfect opportunity to work so she didn't have to think about Quincy and Jason together every five seconds. Even just a few weeks would be enough to remind her why she'd started her travel blog in the first place, and then she could decide what to do for her future.

CHAPTER 6

It had been almost a week since he'd bumped into the woman at the store, but Preston couldn't get her out of his mind. Yet as much as she'd intrigued him, she'd been just passing through, like every other woman he'd thought was remotely interesting and different.

The weather had gone cold, and with all the layers he had to wear to do the chores, he looked like he an Antarctic explorer. He came into the house that morning, blowing on his hands through his gloves and hoping to get some feeling in them soon. The warmth of the mudroom made him sigh with relief. He just needed to get some lunch and thaw out a bit before he had to head back out.

His two youngest brothers were at work and school, and Adam, who worked on several of the machines around the valley, had messaged that he was delayed getting some of the materials Preston had sent him to town for. That would give Preston at least an hour or an hour and a half to rest. He'd been pushing hard, trying to get everything ready before the snowstorm set to hit Coldwater Creek that evening, but he knew it would be worth it to finish now rather than tromping through the large snowdrifts that seemed to last until nearly summer every year.

His phone rang, the tune signaling it was Lauren. "Hey, what's up, sis?"

She giggled, and Preston smiled. It had been a change when she got married to Walker, but it had been nice to have her home for several months after her long few years in Colorado.

"Just thought I'd call and see how things were at the farm. I saw Adam just a bit ago at the hardware store."

"So was he really delayed by weather, or was he just talking to that Susie behind the register?" Preston shook his head, knowing exactly what had held him up.

Again, Lauren laughed. "Definitely Susie. Can I ask you a favor?"

"Oh, so you're not just calling to see how your dear older and most favorite brother is doing, huh? You're just trying to butter me up." He said it all drily, curious what her answer would be to his teasing.

"Please. I can be your favorite sister, but I don't have favorites when it comes to the four of you. You're all so different that I love you for different reasons." Her voice came out more determined than usual, and Preston chuckled, knowing Adam had probably said something similar earlier. It had been a game growing up, trying to get Lauren to admit who was her favorite, and she still held strong even after all these years.

Preston sighed in dramatic fashion. "What is this favor you need from me?"

"Walker and I are leaving for a trip tomorrow, and I was hoping you could stop by every once in a while and make sure everything is okay. We've hired someone to take over the management while we're gone, but I would feel better if she had someone she could call if there's an emergency or anything."

"She? Who is it?" Preston started going through the list of women in the valley, trying to compile the short list of women who had time to manage a lodge and had the skills to do so.

Lauren spoke away from the phone for a few seconds and then came back. "Who did we hire? It's a gal from out of town. She was passing through and offered to work for us while we took a trip since we haven't gone anywhere since our honeymoon."

Preston laughed at that. Lauren had as much of a traveling spirit as he did, and being locked down at the lodge for several months had been a challenge for her, but also a good learning experience. But everyone deserved some time off. "How did you convince Walker to leave?"

"I just said that I had hired someone to take over for us for three weeks and that we were leaving tomorrow. Whether he was on board or not, he was coming."

Preston could picture the defiance in her expression, and he knew that as much as Walker loved the lodge, he loved Lauren even more and was willing to do everything he could to make her happy.

"Yeah, I guess I can check on her every once in a while. What's her name?"

"Ashley Morgan. She'll be staying at the lodge, so just check in maybe after the morning milking." Lauren paused and then said, "Well, maybe a few hours after morning milking. I don't want you to wake any of the guests with your heavy footsteps and loud voice."

Preston grinned. "Oh please. Heavy footsteps. And I talk a lot softer than you might think. I have to yell at the cows so often that it's hard to remember to use my inside voice."

"I'm sure," Lauren said, her voice conveying a smile.

"Okay, well, I've got to get a few more loads of laundry done and then pack us up for our trip to Florida. I booked a secret cruise, so we'll see how that goes. Thanks again, Preston. I owe you."

"Don't worry, I'll hold you to it."

They said goodbye, and he hung up the phone, breathing out a sigh. He tried to picture what the woman would look like, most likely in her forties, probably never married and a drifter. Okay, that wasn't the nicest of descriptions, but that fit the image best. He'd just have to wait to see tomorrow.

He prepped some lunch and ate, heading back outside when Adam finally showed up. If they finished everything on the list today, there wouldn't be as much to do tomorrow, and a trip over to Silver Brook Lodge wouldn't be an inconvenience.

CHAPTER 7

Ashley slept fitfully that night, the excitement and fear washing over her every time she thought about everything she would be in charge of for the next three weeks. Lauren had trained her over the past several days on all the procedures of the lodge, and Ashley was impressed with how organized everything was. There were checklists and procedure sheets for each department, then the things Lauren usually checked on at specific times throughout the day.

This was the biggest job she'd ever been given since she'd graduated high school, and a part of her hoped she would be up for the job. But the rest of her knew she could do it, and with the extra notes she'd taken as Lauren instructed her, she'd at least be able to find most of the answers.

Dressed and ready by seven in the morning, she had just enough time to reassure Lauren that she would be fine. Walker looked a little weary of the whole thing, but she could see that he would do just about whatever he had to for Lauren to be happy. A few weeks of vacation was something this couple definitely needed.

The morning had been slow with only a few people checking out. The woman in charge of the continental breakfast had already checked in that she'd cleaned up everything and was on her way out. And there hadn't been any messages about maintenance in any of the rooms, for which Ashley was grateful. She wasn't sure if she could deal with too much all at the beginning.

The chime over the door sounded when Ashley was in the supply room behind the front desk. She stood from the chair and moved out to the desk, pasting on a smile and preparing herself for a conversation. But when she looked up at the tall man standing before her, all the words disappeared from her brain.

"Chocolate milk man," she said. Then a few seconds later, her brain registered what she'd said, and she pinched her lips together, hoping he would say something.

"I could say the same about you," he said, leaning on the counter only inches away from her. "I take it you're Ashley Morgan?" He raised his eyebrow at the question, but Ashley's eyes couldn't break away from the beautiful blue staring at her.

"Um, I, uh, yep. I'm Ashley. And what's your name?" She looked down, flipping through the registration book so she'd have something else to concentrate on than the fine features of his face.

"Burke. Preston Burke. I'm not a guest, though," he said, gesturing to the pages she was turning. "I'm Lauren's older brother. She asked me to check in on you and make sure things were going okay."

Great! Did Lauren not trust her? The woman had only been gone a total of three hours now, and she already had a family member breathing down Ashley's neck.

As if sensing her thoughts, Preston said, "Don't worry; I'm not here to correct you on anything. Lauren just asked that I make sure you have everything you need and help whenever you need it, provided the emergency doesn't happen around five in the morning or five in the evening."

Curious, Ashley took the bait. "I hope I'm not awake at five in the morning. What happens around those times?"

"Milking. I'm a dairy farmer, and those times are pretty crucial at the farm." He folded his arms on the tall desk, still so close to her she could smell the peppermint of the gum he was chewing.

"Dairy farmer, huh? I have to admit I didn't think that's what you did for a career." Ashley groaned inwardly. She'd met the man a week ago for all of sixty seconds, and she was ashamed to say she'd thought of him way more than that while she'd be in town. And her big mouth had to go blab that to him.

He tilted his head to the side and asked, "Oh, really? What was it you thought I did?"

Glancing around the lodge to allow her brain to form a coherent thought, she finally looked back at him and said, "I guess I thought you were just a country businessman of sorts, or a rancher."

"Businessman I am not. At least, not the city kind. I have to be somewhat savvy on technology to maintain the family business, but I think I'd die if I had to wear a suit every day." Preston grinned, and Ashley sank into the seat, hoping to ease the lack of feeling in her legs. She must have locked them for too long.

"Well, I think things are going well so far. But thanks for checking in. It helps to know I can ask for help if I need it." Ashley smiled at him, her eyes flicking to his lips, and she was grateful for the greater distance she'd put between them. What was it about this guy that had all of her insides humming?

The chime above the door sounded again, and it took a

moment for Ashley to look in that direction. When she did, it seemed as though time had stopped, and she couldn't breathe.

"Oh my goodness! I'm so glad I finally found you," Quincy said, walking around the desk and wrapping her arms around Ashley. The smell of her perfume was so strong Ashley wanted to gag. She looked like she was dressed to head to lunch at a country club instead of winter in a small town.

When she finally pulled back, Ashley couldn't keep the frown from her face. "What are you doing here? I thought I asked for some time." She'd kept her teeth clamped together, hoping Preston wouldn't overhear.

But of course, Quincy couldn't stay quiet about anything. "I was so worried about you. I've been trying to call you for days, but your phone is turned off. I know you said you needed some time, but I was just so worried about you and the future of our business."

Uh-huh. There was the real reason right there.

Quincy turned and noticed Preston for the first time, flashing her signature bright smile at him. "I'm so sorry. Did I interrupt something?"

"No, I was just checking in on Ashley. I'll get going, but call me if you need anything," Preston said, his expression conveying more confusion than anything.

"Why was he checking on you, Ash?" Quincy asked, turning back to Ashley.

Without thinking, she said the first thing that came to her mind. "He was coming to make sure we're ready for our date later."

Her words caused Preston, who was heading for the door, to stop and turn, that eyebrow raising sky high again.

Quincy's mouth dropped open, and she turned back to him as if waiting for the answer. Ashley gave him a pleading look, putting her hands together to signify begging.

"Um, uh, yeah. Just making sure she's ready to go this evening. Six thirty?" Preston asked, looking like he'd just hit an animal on the side of the road and wasn't sure what to do with it.

"Sounds perfect. See you then." Ashley waved and smiled, knowing she'd have to give him an explanation. She waited for him to leave and then thumbed through the numbers in Lauren's contact book. She just hoped her brother's name was there so she could explain everything.

Finding it, she breathed a sigh of relief. Now if only Quincy would leave her in peace.

"You're going out on a date, huh?" Quincy's voice sounded choked, as if the shock was too much.

"Well, it's just a simple dinner. He knew I was new here and asked if I'd like to see the town with him." Ashley was surprised at how well the lies were rolling off her tongue. She should have felt bad about it, but then she remembered what her ex-best friend had done to her.

A thought hit her. Not once had she thought about Jason since Preston had stepped into the lodge. What was that supposed to mean?

"Are you dating him?" Quincy's tone was accusatory, and Ashley could feel the irritation blossoming inside her chest.

Standing, she looked into her cousin's eyes. "Does that matter? I seem to remember being engaged to Jason when you stole him from me. Why do you care about my personal life now? Or were you wanting to steal this one too?"

Quincy took a step back, red moving to her cheeks as though Ashley had slapped her. "I-I-I told you before that I didn't mean to take him away from you."

"I'm trying really hard to be civil about this whole thing, Q, which is why I asked for some time to be alone and figure things out. And you're the last person that gets to judge me about my love life." Ashley turned on her heel and moved into the next room, hoping to get back to the checklist Lauren had left for her. "How did you find me in the first place? I turned my phone off."

Quincy followed her in, her mouth forming an O that let Ashley know she was trying to come up with an explanation on the fly. "I might have looked at your credit statements. You bought a bunch of stuff in Jackson, and when I asked the manager of the hotel you stayed in, he said something about looking south." She paused a moment, staring at her manicure. "The great thing about little towns is that everyone is willing to help you find your cousin."

"I'm sure you played the pity card well, Q." Ashley pulled a ream of paper from the shelf before walking back out of the room and filling the printer with it. Only half of it fit, so she had to return the rest to the shelf.

"But what about the business?" Q asked, following her back to the supply room and then to the front desk again. "We've gotten so many questions about why we haven't posted anything in nearly two weeks, and our readers have a right to get the content they come to us for."

In an even voice, Ashley said with all the calm she could muster, "Then why don't you post something, Q? Maybe about what's going on between us and how it's your fault."

The silence was thick as they both stared at each other. Quincy finally dropped her gaze. "I'll put up something for now, but we need to talk about this, how things are going to work between us now."

"Fine, just not now. I'm working."

Looking around the room, Quincy snorted. "You're taking odd jobs again? I thought we were past all that."

"Q, if you ever want to talk about things again, I suggest you give me some more time to figure things out and what I want from this whole situation. Maybe I'll be able to trust you again, maybe not. But if you keep barging into my life when I ask for space, I'm just going to call everything quits."

Quincy bit her bottom lip, looking as though she was holding back tears. It had been her way to get everything since Ashley could remember, and as Ashley flipped through memory after memory, she realized just how often her cousin did it to get her way.

As if realizing Ashley wasn't going to budge, Quincy finally said, "Fine. I'll be staying at the hotel in Afton. Call me when you're ready to talk."

She turned and walked out, her blonde curls bouncing behind her. Ashley knew she should feel bad about talking to her cousin that way, but she felt satisfied that Quincy could feel just a sliver of the hurt she'd been going through the past several days.

Trying to decide what to do next, Ashley went back to the desk to find Preston's number, hoping he wouldn't think her a total psycho.

CHAPTER 8

*S*till replaying the conversation he'd had with the woman he'd been thinking about since their encounter in the grocery store, Preston wasn't sure he understood what had happened. How had he gone from meeting her for the first time to a sudden date?

His phone rang next to him on the seat, and *Silver Brook Lodge* was running across the screen. He pressed the green button on the dash, allowing the Bluetooth to take the call so he could still drive.

"Hello?"

"Hi, Preston?"

"Yeah."

A quick pause led to the voice continuing. "This is Ashley Morgan, the one you came to check on. I just wanted to say I'm so sorry to put you in that kind of a position, and if you want to cancel our sorta-kinda date, feel free to."

"I'm actually more curious who that woman was and why you lied to her." He turned down the road that led to the farm, grinning as he waited for her response.

"Long story short, she's my cousin and business partner.

There were some disagreements over, uh, some things, and I asked for some time and space to sort it all out. She didn't really listen, and I knew she'd be bugging me all day if I didn't come up with an excuse to get her to leave."

Preston rubbed a hand over his face, noting the stubble he'd forgotten to shave that morning. "I guess I can understand that. I'm happy to help in whatever capacity you need. Lauren would say I'm overprotective after chasing away many of her dates in the past, so if you need help getting rid of what's-her-name, I can do that. But if you don't mind, I'd still like to take you somewhere tonight. Most places close by eight so why don't I pick you up at six thirty or seven? I need to get the milking done before then. Will there be someone there to take over for you?"

"Uh, yes," she said hesitantly. "Marsha Benningfield, it says. Do you want me to meet you somewhere?"

"No, I'll come pick you up."

A pause on the line caused his breath to hitch, wondering if she'd refuse him because of his statement. "Okay. Are you sure you're okay with this?"

Not wanting her to know how interested he was in getting to know her better, he said, "You wouldn't want to be caught in your lie now, would you?"

"No, I guess not."

"Perfect. I'll see you then."

Calculating the time in his head, he'd to get started with the milking a little bit early to get there around that time. He'd just have to stay focused and get done to make it all work.

* * *

With a shower, a fresh shave, and the nicest plaid button-up shirt he owned, Preston did his hair, determining not to wear his cowboy hat tonight. She seemed like a city girl, and while he wasn't going to be changing everything about himself for a woman, most had commented he looked good with his hair done rather than donning a hat.

Adam had agreed to do the milking for the evening since he didn't have any jobs fixing farm equipment around the valley, leaving Preston with more time than he'd expected. The best part about it was that if things didn't go well, he could just drop her back off at the lodge and enjoy a bovine-free evening.

He pulled into the driveway of the lodge and parked. Walking up to the door, he saw that Marsha had already arrived, making him more grateful to the woman than he'd ever been.

"Are you ready?" he asked, leaning on the desk again.

Ashley lifted her pointer finger. "Give me one minute to go change my shirt, and then I will be." She said goodbye to Marsha and took long strides around the corner and up the stairs.

"Taking out the newbie?" Marsha asked with a grin.

Preston looked at her, surprised by the comment. Marsha was one of the middle-aged married women in the valley, and they seemed to form some kind of group to gossip about all the single people. He just didn't want this one spreading too quickly. It was one date, or night out with dinner.

"Lauren asked me to help her out, and I thought it might be a good chance for her to see the town before it gets too cold to want to go out." He stuck his hands into his pants pockets and looked back in the direction of the stairs. He hoped Ashley would hurry so he didn't have to be interrogated.

Marsha made a sound like she didn't believe him. "Have fun tonight. I vote yes for the two of you together."

Preston felt the warmth heat his cheeks, and he hoped it

wasn't visible. He'd managed to avoid the gossipers since he'd quit the rodeo, but now with Easton and Walker married, Marsha just might turn the attention to him, and that was something he didn't want.

"Ready to go?" Ashley asked, standing next to him, buttoning her coat. Preston had been so caught up in his thoughts that he hadn't heard her come down.

"More than you know," he said. Taking a few steps over to the door, he opened it for her and then closed it tightly behind him.

Ashley flashed him a grin. "What's that supposed to mean?"

Preston sighed as he tried to think of the best way to convey everything that had been going through his thoughts in the last few minutes. "Marsha is a great lady, one of the best people in the valley, but she's one of the gossip queens in town."

"Are you worried? We don't have to go out if you don't want." Ashley's neutral expression threw Preston off, and he stopped, trying to sort through his feelings. Maybe she wasn't attracted to him like he was to her.

"I'm fine. This is just dinner with a friend, right?" Preston wished the questioning tone at the end wasn't so high and squeaky.

"Right." She smiled at him, but the action didn't reach her eyes like it normally did, making him even more confused than ever. This girl was good at keeping him on his toes, and he kind of liked that fact.

Shutting the door to his truck after she'd gotten in, he sighed and made his way around to the driver's side, hoping he could at least unravel some of the feelings he had for this girl by the end of the night.

CHAPTER 9

It was about a ten-minute drive from the lodge to Afton, and Ashley enjoyed the time in Preston's warm truck. She would have to order a warmer coat if she were to stay here much longer, as the one she owned was nothing more than a parka. The cool wind seemed to blow through it as though she weren't wearing anything to keep warm.

Preston pulled along the curb next to what looked like a diner. As he opened her door, she could smell charbroiled meat and realized how hungry she was.

"It's not much, but they make some good food," Preston said, coming up alongside her as she stared at the sign above the restaurant. The sound of his voice made her turn and study his face for several seconds.

She'd seen something in his eyes back at the lodge when she'd suggested they not go out, and she could only hope it was the same panicked feeling she'd felt at the thought of not going out with him. She'd been so excited for most of the day, counting down the hours until she could see him again. A stranger. She was losing it.

Or was that a sign that things between her and Jason had fizzled out long ago? Because she either couldn't remember feeling butterflies with her ex-fiancé or it had just been so long since she'd felt like that toward him. But after a quick internal examination, there was no guilt. Maybe something had broken once she'd found out about their betrayal.

"It smells delicious." She took a few steps forward, and he hurried around her, opening the door for her to enter. Her mouth decided to react on its own again, and she said, "Are all of you country boys this gentlemanly? Because someone should have told me about that years ago."

A wave of different emotions played along his face, and Ashley stepped into the small diner that had been decorated in a fifties theme. A jukebox stood next to the entrance near the hostess stand.

A young girl came walking out from the back with a few quick steps and stood next to the stand. "Preston and date?" Her eyebrows raised as she looked at Preston with curiosity.

"This is Ashley Morgan. She's taking over for Lauren at the lodge while she and Walker are gone." Turning to Ashley, he said, "Ashley, this is Molly McBride, Walker's youngest sister."

Ashley stretched out her hand. "It's so nice to meet you."

"How long have you been working here, Molly?" Preston asked as the girl grabbed two menus and directed them to follow her.

"About three days. Mom said I should probably get a job to pay for all my extracurricular activities, and they had an opening here."

Preston waited for Ashley to slide into the booth across from him and then said, "Your brother didn't have a job for you at the lodge?"

"I figured I'd try something else first. Today's special is the California burger with fries and a shake. I'll let you two look over the menu, and I'll be back to take your order." She smiled at both of them before moving into the back room.

With a sly smile, Preston leaned over the table and said, "She's got a crush on one of the cooks."

"Smart girl. Nothing like forced time together to see if he feels the same." Ashley chuckled and so did Preston for a few seconds. But as she looked over the menu, she realized how much that sounded like her current situation. There seemed to be so many hidden secrets when it came to Preston that she wondered if it was the curiosity that kept her intrigued or if it was just rebound feelings. Because she'd never felt so at ease when she was with Jason.

After Molly came back and took their orders, Ashley leaned forward, a million questions wanting to dive out of her mouth for the handsome guy before her. It was the first time she felt like she had a time limit on learning things about him, and if she missed that chance, she'd always regret it.

"So, tell me about your farm. Has it been in your family for a few generations?"

Preston nodded. "Four. And I think that's why my dad hasn't wanted to give up on it completely yet."

"Is it not profitable?" Ashley bit her tongue after the comment, realizing how personal it had been. "I'm sorry. I'm always curious about people's careers, and while I've done a couple of short stints working on a farm, I don't have extensive knowledge about them."

"You're fine," Preston said, taking a sip of water. "It's profitable enough, but it's not what I'd always imagined doing with my life."

Seeing that she'd intertwined her fingers before her, she pulled her hands onto her lap and said, "What did you want to do?"

Preston leaned back, his arm resting on the back of the

booth. "I always thought I'd do the rodeo circuit until I got too old and then I'd figure out something from there. Raise horses for the rodeo or for racing or something like that. Dairy farming was very low on the list."

"So, what changed your mind?"

He paused and took another long swig of water, his blue eyes staring at her like he was trying to decide on something. "My mother was diagnosed with a rare form of cancer. So I came home and did what I could to help out around the farm while my dad had to run her to Idaho Falls and down to Salt Lake for tests. My youngest brothers are still pretty young, so I had to take on a lot of responsibility, which was fine because we were all worried about Mom."

He paused, swallowing hard. "Once she passed, I felt bad because I was sort of relieved. She was no longer in pain, and I could go back to doing what I loved. But several months later, my dad had a stroke, and it paralyzed his right side."

Ashley gasped and slapped her hand over her mouth. "I'm sorry. That's so hard."

"He's managing now, but it's still hard for him to do a lot. The farm is the one source of income for the family, and as much as I don't like doing the same thing day after day, I know how much it helps my dad and my siblings have a normal life." He paused a second and grinned. "What brought you to Coldwater Creek? Are you on vacation from some boring desk job?"

Feigning offense, Ashley rested her hand on her chest. "Do I look like I'd survive a boring desk job?"

When Preston chuckled and shook his head, she laughed with him. "It's funny you say 'on vacation' because that's kind of what I built my business out of. My cousin, the one you met today, and I ran a travel website and blog where we chronicled our adventures in certain resorts and different destinations."

"Why do you say it like you don't do it anymore?"

"Because I'm trying to decide—"

The door opened, and a familiar voice said, "What are you two doing here?"

Ashley turned to see Quincy and Jason walking through the door. She had brought Jason with her? She had some nerve. How could she be so heartless?

Closing her eyes, Ashley rested her hands over them, hoping this was just some bad nightmare and that the real date with Preston wouldn't be plagued by people from her past.

Groaning, she said, "Seriously? Why come here of all places?"

"There aren't many options in this small town, and a lot of people referred us here for the food," Quincy said, putting her hand on her hip.

"Jason, I didn't realize you were in town as well." Ashley's words were full of bitterness, and she wished she could just grab Preston and run out the door.

"Quincy thought a trip here would do us good. Who's your friend?"

Ashley turned to look at Preston, wondering what to say to her ex-fiancé. Without thinking too much, she blurted out, "This is Preston Burke, my boyfriend."

Jason took a step back, as if hit with the title. "You-you already have a boyfriend?"

"It wasn't like you waited long, or waited at all, before breaking off your engagement to me." She folded her arms over her chest and stared at the spot on the wall just behind Jason's head. It helped her cool down a bit before she said anything she regretted.

Molly came out then, asking how many were in their party, and escorted them to a table next to the front window. It was then that Ashley looked up at Preston, the look of shock and horror in his expression causing her to backpedal. Her mouth had gotten her into trouble again.

CHAPTER 10

*P*reston's mind kept the words running around in a loop, and he wasn't sure what to make of them. "This is Preston Burke, my boyfriend."

He wasn't sure what had thrown him off guard more, that an almost-stranger had given him the title or that it had been so long since he'd had a girlfriend that he kind of liked it. And from the little he knew about her, it made him want to get to know her even more. A girl who traveled the world and got paid for it? If only he'd thought about something like that to both help out his family and get the adventure his soul needed.

Ashley reached over and rested her hand on his forearm, her eyes as round as the sugar container on the table. "I'm so sorry. I don't know what got into me with that. I can go tell them it's not true." She moved to slide out of the booth, but Preston caught hold of her wrist.

"Just hold on a minute," he said, trying to figure out what to do with the situation. "Give me a little more background on your relationship with those two." He pointed to the two people who were more connected to Ashley than she'd let on earlier that day. He suddenly wanted to know the whole story.

Fiddling with the napkin, Ashley said, "Quincy and I started our website when we were just out of high school. Well, I should say we started traveling after graduation, and then with a ton of pictures and blogs being all the rage, we decided to post them. We got a lot of traffic and slowly started getting sponsors and stuff. She's always been the scheduler and public relations person, while I took care of the rest of it: the social media, the marketing, etc."

She let out a long breath, seeming reluctant to continue. "About four years ago, we needed to hire an IT guy to maintain our site, so we found Jason. He and I started dating a year later, and then he proposed to me about eighteen months ago. We were set to get married this Christmas."

Preston saw the emotions creep into her face, her eyes welling with tears. He wasn't sure what to do. Did he reach out and hug her, even though they'd only known each other a few hours? He glanced over to the couple near the window and wondered if throwing a fist or two would help her feel better. Before that idea took hold, she took a deep breath and kept talking.

"About two weeks ago, the two of them sat me down and said they're in love and that Jason was breaking things off with me." She used her ring finger to wipe a tear from the corner of her eye and sniffed. There was a slight discoloration there where the ring must have been. "We had the venue booked, the invitations designed, my dress ready for the final fitting…everything."

"I'm so sorry, Ashley. I didn't know. What can I do to help?"

A deep laugh came from her, and Preston could hear the sadness there. Reaching out, he clasped one of her hands in his.

"Thanks for listening. These last two weeks have been really eye-opening for me, and part of me is relieved we aren't going through with things. The other part just feels betrayed, like if I can't trust my cousin/business partner and my fiancé/employee, can I trust anyone?" Her words were down to a whisper, and Preston had to lean in to hear her.

Molly appeared at the table, and when she saw Ashley crying, panic settled into her features. Before she could say anything, Preston said, "Can you pack up our order? We'll take it to go."

Within a few minutes, they'd paid the bill and taken their hamburgers and shakes out to his truck.

"I'm so sorry," Ashley said, pulling at a loose string on her jacket. "I shouldn't have broken down or even burdened you with all my lame problems."

"What are you talking about? If I'd had something like that happen to me, I know I wouldn't be handling it quite as well as you have. I probably would have thrown a punch or something." He was glad when that got a hint of a smile from her.

She shook her head. "I just don't get why they won't leave me alone. And the fact that she brought Jason here is odd. He doesn't like to leave the comfort of Texas if he doesn't have to."

Preston frowned. "This might be an odd question, then, but why did you want to marry him? It sounds like you love traveling and taking new adventures. You were okay with someone who didn't want to do that with you?"

Ashley bit the side of her bottom lip and was silent for some moments. "I never really thought about it like that. I guess I figured I could change that about him. But it was like pulling teeth to get him to go anywhere. I had to basically hold his hand to get his passport for what should have been our honeymoon to the Bahamas, which I had to plan. Well, that's not completely true. The resort was going to pay for the trip as long as we promoted it. Always work."

Leaning his head back against the window of his truck, Preston let out a deep laugh. How strange was it for a girl who loved to travel to be stuck with someone who didn't want to go anywhere? Not that if Ashley were with him anything would be different. He was still strapped to the cows and their milking schedule. As much as he would have loved to do what she was doing, he couldn't get too caught up in a daydream.

"I know. A lot of things have been more in focus ever since they told me. I just, well, thank you for getting me out of there. And thank you for listening. You don't know how much I needed that tonight." She took a bite of her burger and dabbed at the corners of her mouth with a napkin. "Somewhere along the line, things got a little skewed, and I don't know if I can ever go back to how it was before, or how to make it fun again."

"Well, the good thing is, you don't have to have all the answers tonight. Take time to enjoy it here. Maybe it will help spark some of that old excitement about your career."

"Coming from the guy who has to deal with cows all day."

Raising his hands in surrender, Preston said, "I know, I know. I'm basically a walking hypocrite, but it's all for the end goal of my family."

They chatted for quite a while longer, and even though Preston told himself things could never work out between them, it seemed his heart was no longer listening. But maybe he could enjoy this time, enjoy the few weeks she was in town, and then she'd disappear, just a distant memory. He might as well live vicariously through her stories to get him through the long winter ahead.

If there had ever been anything between her and Jason, Ashley was sure it was nothing more than platonic at this point. She'd never had someone so caring and considerate as Preston in her life, and the fact that he'd saved her from their stares and whispered conversations meant so much. And then the comment about Jason being anti-traveling caused her to think long and hard.

Why had she thought she was in love with Jason for all that time? Was it because he was some sort of stability in what was a never-ending vacation life? He'd always been there when she came home from a trip, had been that one steady constant. But she didn't want to travel by herself or with her cousin for the rest of her life. She wanted her husband and kids right alongside her when they discovered a new hiking trail or a delicious soda shop.

Preston seemed like he would jump at the chance to travel, and the more she got to know him, the more she felt like they were connected somehow. She couldn't imagine losing her mother so early in life and then having all that responsibility of taking care of younger siblings, sacrificing what he wanted to do for what would benefit the entire family.

She'd never met her father. Her own mother lived in Chicago, and it had been way longer than it should have since Ashley had last visited. She'd need to visit before the year was out, and maybe the holidays would be perfect for that. To get away from Texas, away from the thought of a failed wedding, and just enjoy some time to herself with her mom for a few days.

The more she thought about it, the more she realized her words about the canceled wedding being more of a relief than anything were spot on. She'd been so excited to be engaged and planning the wedding, but to be with Jason forever and ever at this point seemed more like drudgery than anything. It was the betrayal that hurt the worst.

I had a lot of fun tonight. I hope you sleep well, and let me know if there's something I can do for you.

Ashley grinned wider than she'd done in quite some time, that giddy feeling taking over as she read and reread the text from Preston.

Thank you. You too. Let me know if you need me to take one of your milking shifts.

Maybe coming to Coldwater Creek had been an answer to an unspoken prayer. She was coming to like this place even more—and a certain someone in it.

CHAPTER 12

The next day came around faster than Ashley had hoped since she'd stayed up late reviewing several of the details from the night before over and over again, analyzing like a teenage girl with her crush. She knew she needed to distance her heart from Preston, but she couldn't seem to do that. She wanted to text him, to call him about every little dumb thing that happened throughout the day, something she'd never done with Jason.

By midday, she was feeling like everything was working out and even thinking about what a future here could look like for her. What would she do for work if she didn't do the travel website anymore? It was something she needed to think about, and she just hoped Quincy would avoid stopping by anytime soon, and give her time to think it over.

"We are all done cleaning up the rooms for the day, Ashley," Laura, the head cleaner, said as she walked up to the front desk.

"Perfect. We have a few new check-ins coming soon, so that will help." Ashley bent over the small list she'd written for herself today, crossing off *cleaning* on it.

"I hear you've tamed the bachelor of Coldwater Creek." The playful tone of the young woman's voice caught Ashley off guard.

Leaning a bit closer, Ashley asked, "Excuse me. What?"

"Preston Burke. I heard earlier today that the two of you are dating. There are a few broken hearts in the valley, but he's a good one." Laura winked as she turned away and walked toward the door.

Ashley tried to find the words to call her back, but the girl was already gone. Her heart beat faster and faster as she thought about what that meant and hoped Preston didn't think she was some crazy girl because she'd come in like a twister and thrown off his entire life.

Picking up her phone, she dialed his number, hoping he would pick up.

"Hey, how are things going today?" The smooth sound of his voice made the anxious knots in her stomach dissolve, and she sat down in the chair, taking a deep breath before she had to ruin the feeling.

"Well, the cleaning lady just informed me that we're dating and the whole valley pretty much knows about it. I'm so sorry I got you into this mess." She leaned forward and set her head on the desk, raising it a bit and then dropping it again so her forehead smacked onto the top.

"Hey, hey," Preston soothed. "What if we just go with it for a bit?"

"Pretend we're dating?" Ashley sat up straight. She'd be able to save face with Jason and Quincy, but what would that benefit him?

His deep laugh came through the line, and Ashley was ready to hear his proposition. "To be honest, it will be doing me the favor. Hearing your adventures helps me get through my boring life, and now that people have seen us out together, I'll be the target of all the set-ups if it's known we aren't actually dating. I don't care to be forced out on a date with Mrs. Murphy's granddaughter again."

Ashley couldn't hold back a laugh at that. "I can only imagine how painful that was since I don't know who Mrs. Murphy is."

"Just an old do-gooder woman who thinks being single is the plague of the earth. She's been trying to find me a wife for at least three years."

"And when was the last time you had a date before we went out last night?" she asked, teasing him but wanting to know the answer at the same time.

There was a quick pause, and Ashley overhead a few numbers being whispered through the line. "About a year."

"A year? I don't feel bad for you, then. It sounds like the women of this town don't worry about you too much."

"Please," he began. "It's been a year since I agreed. That doesn't mean there haven't been plenty of offers."

"Okay, for the sake of your bachelorhood sanity, I agree to be your fake girlfriend. But we need to come up with some ground rules."

Preston cleared his throat. "Ground rules? Are we in high school?"

"No, but it's nice to have some boundaries so we're comfortable, don't you think?"

A long pause seemed to beat through to her ear, and Ashley pulled the phone back to make sure the call hadn't disconnected.

When Preston's voice came back on a bit rushed, he said, "Hey, Ash, I'm sorry. I have to run and take care of a hole in the roof of one of the hay barns. We'll talk later, okay?"

"No problem. Good luck!" She hung up the phone and rested it on her chest, wondering why the swarm of butterflies in her stomach was so excited over a fake boyfriend.

"You do like him, don't you?" Marsha asked, coming up to the desk.

"I don't know what you mean." Ashley sat up, hoping the woman hadn't heard too much of the conversation.

Marsha came around the desk and sat in the empty chair, a mischievous grin on her face. "I heard a rumor today that you two were dating, but I didn't think it could happen that fast, especially not with Preston Burke. But it seems like you two click a lot better than some of the other ones around this valley. Just be gentle on him. He's been through a lot."

Her words seemed to smack Ashley with a good dose of reality. What was she thinking? She'd already told herself numerous times not to worry about him and that she wouldn't be able to fully commit after the hurt she'd felt at Jason's betrayal.

But then she thought of the little things, the open doors and the ease she had talking with him, and part of her wanted to give it a chance, at least for the short time she'd be in town.

She left the lodge, hoping to see some more of the valley before complete darkness set in. Driving north, she was surprised at the beauty held between the two mountain ranges, the tan fields and snaking river between making for some great pictures. This place was like a balm to her soul, something she needed after so long of the hustle and bustle.

Taking one of the turnoffs, she drove the car around some winding roads until it opened up into another beautiful valley. She'd heard someone say that everything from the town south of Afton all the way up to Alpine was part of Coldwater Creek, and the scene before her must be part of that.

Not knowing exactly where she'd gone, she turned north, seeing an old church and then several small houses spread out along a large block. Fields stretched out on either side, such a change from the beaches she was so used to visiting. After making several turns to the right and left, she found herself at the end of a road, and a large farmhouse stood before her. It looked older but still in good repair, with several trees lining the sides of it.

The road turned right in front of it, and as she slowly made her way on the road, she recognized Preston's large truck parked in the driveway. Making a snap decision, she decided to pull in, not know what she'd say when she knocked on the door.

She stood on the porch and hesitated. What was she doing here? Just because he'd taken her out didn't mean she needed to come bugging him already. As she turned to walk back to her car, she heard the squeak of a door behind her. Great, she was caught.

"May I help you?" a voice similar to Preston's asked.

Turning around, Ashley felt her cheeks heat up. "Well, um, I saw Preston's truck in the drive and thought I'd stop by and say hello." Why couldn't she think of something more eloquent to say?

"He's out in the milking barn. You can come through here." The young man had similar features to Preston, but his build was much leaner and his eyes a dark brown. He opened the screen door and gestured for her to follow him through.

Part of her wanted to turn around and run to her car. They were just pretending to be in a relationship, but that was mostly for the eyes of the town and her ex-fiancé.

After looking at the young man again, she took a step forward, moving past the threshold and into the neat farmhouse. Glancing around quickly as she followed Preston's presumed brother, she was surprised at how tidy everything was. Even the room she was staying in at the lodge didn't look like this, with all her belongings strewn everywhere.

They walked through the kitchen and a large mudroom before exiting the house.

"I take it you're one of Preston's brothers?" she asked, trying to feel less self-conscious about barging into their world.

"I'm Seth, the youngest." He gave her a small smile and waited for her to walk beside him as they moved toward a large outbuilding. There were several small potholes and puddles, which Seth helped her miss by pointing them out.

Pulling open a door, he waved her through, much like Preston had several times now. Whatever their mother taught them, it had sure stuck.

The sound inside the building was loud, making it hard to think for several seconds until she adjusted a bit. After a minute or two, they found Preston just outside the building, working to move several cows inside the shed.

He looked up and saw her, a mixture of surprise and happiness dancing across his face. With a quick wave, he showed two fingers as if to say he just needed a couple minutes.

Seth leaned over and said next to her ear, "Sorry, I've got a lot of homework to catch up on. I'll leave you here if that's okay."

Ashley smiled at him. "Of course. I totally get it. Good luck with that."

She turned her attention back to Preston and watched as he moved the animals into their stalls, wiping their udders with a cloth and then attaching what looked like suction cups to the teats. He turned on a machine and then walked over to her, gently guiding her back away from the building.

"This is a surprise. What brings you here?" Preston asked, using his fingers to comb his hair down. His lips twisted to the side, giving him a goofy expression, something Ashley loved. She wasn't someone who could be completely serious her entire life, and now that she thought of it, there hadn't been too many times when she'd heard Jason all-out laugh about something.

"I was out for a drive and recognized your truck. I thought I'd see your farm if you had time." Her heart rate sped up awaiting his answer.

Preston looked back at the field. "I can definitely give you a tour if you don't mind waiting a few more minutes. I'm almost done with the milking for tonight, and then I'm free." He smiled at her. "Just a minute. Let me check on this group."

Ashley watched him walk away, enjoying the view as he went. After several seconds, she groaned. Was she a glutton for punishment? She'd lose her heart to this guy and then have to leave soon when Lauren and Walker returned from their trip. She'd never been good at staying in one place, but as Preston emerged once more, she couldn't help but push those thoughts away, getting lost in the moment.

"Can I help?" she blurted out, surprising herself.

"Of course. Let me get you some overalls and boots. You won't want to ruin your work clothes." He pointed to her black pants and small heels, and Ashley realized how over-dressed she was for a farm setting.

He strode inside and grabbed a pair of pink overalls and matching rubber boots. Handing them to her, he said, "Just pull those up over your clothes. I wouldn't suggest wearing the heels inside the boots, though."

They both chuckled at that.

Ashley slipped one foot into the overalls and then another, pulling the straps up over her shoulders. As she worked to pull on the boots, she said, "It's pretty impressive that you just had a selection of overalls and boots that fit me, especially the color."

His face sobered, and he said, his voice one of reverence, "Those were my mother's. You're about the same size, so I figured they'd work. Lauren's work clothes might look like you're waiting for a flood since she's so short."

Ashley froze, not sure if she should continue wearing them or not. "I can just help you in my regular clothes."

Preston held up a hand and shook his head. "No, I'm sure she would be happy to have someone using them. She always had a flair for pink, and we all laughed the first time she came out to the barn with those on."

His eyes turned a bit glassy, and Ashley took a step forward, resting her hand on his forearm. "You miss her, don't you?"

Preston's bottom lip quivered, and he nodded, a small tear escaping down his cheek. He opened his mouth as if to say something but closed it again.

Without thinking, Ashley reached up and wiped at the tear, feeling the bristles of his facial hair against her skin. His eyes were far off now, and she reached her arms around his middle, pulling him close.

It took several seconds for his arms to go around her, but she'd never felt safer than right then. Not that there was anything to be protected from, but it was a feeling she'd never realized she needed.

They stood there for several minutes, Ashley breathing in the smell of his cologne mixed with outdoor animals. When a bunch of alarms went off, he pulled back, wiping at his eyes.

"Sorry about that," he said, blinking a few times.

"Life stinks sometimes, but if I can help out with a hug and a listening ear, I'm here." She smiled at him and felt a zing of satisfaction when he returned it.

How was it possible to be so close to someone she'd known for such a short while? She wanted him to tell her everything, all about his past, in the hopes that she'd fully understand why he was the man he was today. But then again, that kind of intensity probably wasn't needed right now, or ever.

She'd enjoy her time with Preston and then figure out the next chapter of her life.

CHAPTER 13

*P*reston wanted to kick himself for getting emotional around Ashley. He hadn't thought much of it when he'd grabbed the overalls and boots, but when she put them on, she reminded him of his mother, and the emotions had broken through the wall he'd thought was strong enough to hold it all back.

The fact that she'd shown up there after she finished managing at the lodge was both surprising and exciting. And the fact that she'd sought him out when she didn't have to made his mind spin with possibilities. As much as he tried to keep her at arm's length, he wished he could just keep her close and take away some of her pain, just as she had by embracing him.

"Okay, this is where we do all the milking." He put his arms out and waved them around to signify the area.

"I bet the machines help things go faster," she said, raising her voice to be heard over the sound.

Preston nodded. "That's true. I've complained a time or two, wishing it would milk the animals faster, but this is still easier than doing each cow separately."

"Where do the tubes take the milk to?" Ashley asked, pointing to the black tubes running up near the ceiling of the barn.

"To a large tank where we keep all the milk. We supply the cheese factory in town with all of its fresh milk. They also use it to make everything else you can imagine with the dairy."

Ashley smiled. "I'm a fan of cheese. I didn't know there were special factories for all that."

"The one factory closed down a while ago, but another one was just finished. How did you think the cheese in the store was made?" Preston chuckled.

Ashley blushed. "I guess I never gave it too much thought. But I will have to stop in and see it while I'm in town."

The sounds beeped, signaling the end of the cycle for several of the cows. He began unhooking them, and Ashley bent down next to him, watching the whole process. He walked her through it and at one point turned, bringing their faces so close he could easily close the inch distance between them and kiss her.

His breath hitched, and he turned back to finish unlatching the cow from the machine. If he was going to kiss her, it wasn't going to be here in the milking barn.

Her words, "While I'm in town," kept echoing through his mind, and he knew he was falling faster than he should. Of course, it would be his luck to find a girl he was attracted to and interested in and she'd be some sort of world traveler. But the way she'd offered to get in and help him made him wonder what it would be like to have her by his side always.

None of the girls in town had ever offered to come help with the chores; they'd always waited for him to be showered and clean-shaven. Ashley didn't seem to mind about any of it, as though everything was a new adventure for her. But would it be the same after twenty, forty, sixty years of this?

Once they finished up with the last group of cows, Preston herded them all back out to the pasture, glad he was done for the evening.

"Are you ready for that tour?" he asked.

"Of course. This is all so fascinating. I'll definitely remember this every time I drink milk or eat cheese." She grinned at him, sending his insides into a puddle.

He walked beside her, pointing out the different buildings they had on the farm and then showing her the extent of the acreage his family owned.

"This valley is so beautiful. What was it like to grow up here?" Ashley asked, her eyes searching the horizon. Was she looking beyond the mountains to her next destination?

"I guess just how most kids look at it. There was always a lot of work and just a little time to play. But every once in a while, I get that feeling like, 'Wow! I can't believe I live in a place like this.' That's usually in the height of spring when things are green. I'm really good at complaining about the long winters."

His words caused her to laugh loudly, her head tipped back and eyes pinched shut. Preston joined in, feeling more relaxed there on the farm than he had in quite a while. When their laughter died down, he debated whether or not to ask the question on his mind.

"So, have you decided what you'll do about your website yet? I mean, I know you wanted time to think about it. I was just, um, curious." He tried to make his expression casual, like he had no worries one way or the other, but the selfish part of him wanted her to say she was thinking about staying in Coldwater Creek forever.

Ashley shook her head. "I haven't figured that out just yet. I've thought a lot about it, and I guess I need to just have a talk with Quincy and Jason and see what we can do to work things out. I mean, this place has given me a great perspective on my life, and there are some things I need to put my foot down on. Traveling is still something I love to do, but I'd like more downtime in between. It's been go, go, go for over eight years, and I just want to enjoy places a little more and not have to feel like I have to share everything about it to get paid."

"Maybe you should get a place here in the valley, and it could be where you could escape to when you're between trips." His voice sounded more hopeful than he wanted it to, but he shook it off, knowing it was all just wishful thinking.

Ashley smiled at that. "I wouldn't mind. This place is beautiful and would be a nice change from Texas."

They moved around the rest of the farm, and when they made it back to the farmhouse, Preston wasn't sure if he should bring her inside and introduce her to his family. Their relationship was a fake one after all, and maybe keeping them out of the mix would be easier when things were over.

She took off the overalls and boots and handed them to him, and he walked her to her car and opened the door for her. "It was fun having you stop by, and thanks again for helping me out with the chores. It was definitely more fun with a pretty girl next to me." His eyes went wide, and he wiggled his jaw, hoping she didn't read too much into it and get scared off.

"I had a blast." She paused a moment. "Thanks for taking the time to show me everything. I'm always curious about different careers and how people live. Maybe that's why I love traveling so much, so I can see the varieties in life."

She said goodbye and drove away, but Preston stood in the driveway long after her car was visible. He wasn't sure what he was going to do, but he kept hoping for more time. Something that was sure to come to an end.

CHAPTER 14

The next few days were busy with several new check-ins, and Ashley loved asking each person or couple where they were from and what had brought them to this sleepy little town. The answers ranged from a family get-together all the way to stopping through on their way to Canada.

She'd talked to Preston a few times since she stopped by the farm but hadn't had a chance to see him. He always seemed to be at the front of her mind, and with any lull, she found herself thinking about him or analyzing one of their previous interactions.

Tuesday night, she went to bed a little later as Marsha had to call in because her daughter was sick. Bernie, the maintenance man, headed home at normal time, saying everything was in order and he'd be back in the morning. But at eleven that night, Ashley was alerted to the fact that a pipe had burst and a toilet was overflowing in one of the outer cabins.

It took a minute to shake off the deep sleep she'd finally slipped into, but she was up and dressed in under a minute, rushing out to cabin number eight.

"Are you all right?" she asked the couple standing outside the cabin. They looked like they'd thrown all their belongings into their suitcases and were holding a blanket around the two of them.

"Just glad none of our stuff got soaked," the man said, pulling his wife closer to his side. "I got up to use the toilet, and when I flushed, it just started gushing water."

Ashley tried to hide a smile, knowing that laughing in front of a client wasn't going to equal a good review for the lodge. "Well, let's get you inside. I'll find a place for you to get settled, and we'll go from there."

She ushered them into the main lodge and hurried to make a cup of hot chocolate to warm them while they waited. It was just below freezing outside, and she knew a hot beverage would help as she got them resituated.

She dialed Bernie, but after several attempts and no answer, she clicked over to Preston's name and pressed the send button.

"Hello?" His voice came out muffled like he'd been sleeping for a while. Glancing at the clock, Ashley grimaced. He usually went to bed by nine so he could function when he had to get up and milk in the morning.

"Oh, I'm so sorry! Go back to sleep. I'll figure something—"

"Ashley, I'm up. What's wrong? Are you okay?" Preston's deep voice sent a soothing sensation through her chest.

Taking a deep breath, she relayed what had happened with the cabin and that she couldn't get in touch with Bernie.

"I'll be there in ten," he said.

"Thank you so much. I'm not the best at fixing leaks or spills or whatever." She bit her bottom lip, trying to tamp down the excitement she felt at him coming to see her. Well, to fix the cabin.

After hanging up the phone, she logged into the computer

and checked the room status. How had she not noticed they were completely booked that afternoon?

Her mind started spinning, trying to come up with the perfect solution to the situation. The couple would be checking out the next day.

Walking into the large great room, she stood before them. "Okay, if you'll give me about fifteen minutes, I can get a room ready for you that shouldn't have any leaks. Will that work?"

The couple nodded, and after turning on the large television to distract them, Ashley ran upstairs, taking them two at a time.

She pulled her luggage from the closet and started chucking things inside. The pile of clothes that sat on one side of her bed was thrown in, along with the several pairs of shoes scattered about the room. She stripped the bed and took the load downstairs to the laundry room, where she grabbed a fresh set as well as the bucket of cleaning supplies from the maid's closet.

By the time she'd scrubbed the bathroom and made the bed, it was closer to thirty minutes that the couple had been waiting.

"I'm so sorry, you two," Ashley said, wiping away a few beads of sweat as she came down the stairs. "I've got it all ready for you upstairs. Let me get your bags for you."

The woman allowed her to carry her suitcase while the man hefted the larger one up the stairs. Ashley was strong, but she was glad she didn't have to carry it all the way to the room.

"Okay, this is the room you'll stay in, and let me know if you need anything or would like an extra night stay because of the inconvenience." She smiled and left them, trudging down the stairs. Exhaustion piled onto her shoulders, the effect of the adrenaline wearing off.

Seeing her bag at the bottom of the stairs, she moved it into the employee hallway, not wanting any other guests to have to move around it should they be up extra early.

The back door opened, and Ashley's pulse shot up. She'd forgotten to lock it once she let the couple in. Taking steps as quietly as possible, she walked to the hallway and peeked around the corner.

"Hey," Preston said, only inches away from her.

She jumped, nearly hitting her head against the corner of the wall. "Hi," she said, trying to act casual. "I was sure you were some kind of serial killer because I'd forgotten to lock the door."

Raising his hands, Preston gave her a wide smile. "Just me. I got the toilet to stop flooding and cleaned up as much water as I could. I'm pretty sure Walker keeps a fan in their room, so I'm going to take it out there and hope it helps dry things out. Nothing like clogging a toilet to make for an interesting night," he said with a chuckle.

"So it wasn't a broken pipe. I think that's why the couple was so chill. He looked somewhat guilty, and I couldn't really call him out on it."

"Did you have a room for them?" Preston asked, glancing around as if they were still waiting.

Ashley nodded. "I may have given them my room."

Preston frowned. "Where are you going to sleep?"

Taking a few steps into the great room, Ashley waved her hands over the couch, as if she were some kind of game show host. "This will be my spot for the night."

"You could always sleep in Lauren and Walker's room. I'm sure they wouldn't mind." Preston pointed in the direction of the master suite.

"No, it's only for one night, and I'll be totally fine. I've slept in the most random places: airports, buses…It will just be another fun story to tell." She smiled and giggled when he looked like he didn't quite believe her.

He grabbed the fan from his sister's room and disappeared out the door. Ashley made another cup of hot chocolate, not sure what else to offer him for coming to her rescue.

"Thank you," he said, accepting the cup from her once he came back in. He'd removed his winter coat and boots, and his cheeks and the tip of his nose were rosy from the cold.

"Come sit down and warm up," Ashley said, adding another log onto the fire and stoking it a bit. The warmth seeped through her clothes, and she looked down, just now realizing she'd been traipsing around in an oversized sweatshirt and her unicorn pajama pants.

Preston sat on the couch, and Ashley pulled one of the warm blankets over with her and sat on the cushion next to him with her legs curled underneath her.

"Thank you for coming to aid me. I didn't really look at the clock before I called you, and when I heard your voice, I—"

"Ashley, it's fine. I'm glad you called. I would've felt bad if you'd had to figure it all out by yourself." He took a long draw from his cup and stood, disappearing into the kitchen. Was he leaving already? Then again, he did have to get up in a few hours to milk. But the selfish part of Ashley wanted him to stay with her.

Within a few seconds, he reappeared, walking over to the fire and stoking it once again. As he stood, he rubbed his hands together, the corner of his mouth turning up.

"It's a cold one out." He hesitated before sitting on the couch a few inches closer to her. The smell of clean soap drifted in her direction.

"That's why we have blankets," Ashley said with a grin. She lifted the edge of her blanket closest to him, and he scooted over, pulling it across him. Ashley felt an added warmth almost immediately; although, she wasn't sure if it was because of the stoked fire or the fact that Preston was sitting so close to her.

He leaned his head back against the couch, a slow smile taking hold. Within a few seconds, he'd taken her hand in his, interlocking their fingers. She had to look down again, surprised by the tingles coursing through her palm.

"What are you smirking about?" Ashley said, trying to quell the waver of excitement in her voice.

"Just the fact that this is kind of where Walker and Lauren's story began. Sitting in front of the fire after her car slid into one of the fences out front during a blizzard. They were trapped in the lodge for a few days before snowplows cleared the snow away from the roads."

Ashley glanced around the beautiful room with pictures of landscapes in rustic frames positioned throughout it. She tried to calm her heart as she thought of his first sentence. Did he mean this was the beginning of their story together? So much of her wanted that, and yet it was a little bit daunting to have such strong feelings for someone she'd known less than a week.

She and Jason had only started dating after knowing each other a year, which was how Ashley usually liked things. Her life was unpredictable when it came to work and where she would be located in the next week or month, but having a somewhat predictable relationship with Jason had its appeal at the beginning. She'd seen her mother's relationships come and go for years since her father's death when she was a young girl, which probably played into that one bit of security.

But she hadn't realized that liking someone could come with such intense feelings, making her feel like she was on top of the world while at the same time clinging to the idea of how to make it last longer than her allotted time in Coldwater Creek.

"Penny for your thoughts." Preston's eyes were turned to her, and she smiled, hoping her cheeks didn't give away what she was feeling.

"I was just thinking about this place. It's amazing. This town is amazing. There's the feeling of home here. I guess I haven't felt that in a long time, longer than I can even remember."

Preston grinned. "Some of the older ladies are a little too motherly. But for someone who sees all the sights, I can imagine this would seem like a good place to slow down."

"I wish I could take you to some of the places I've been, to show you how incredible the lakes and beaches can be. But then I think of your life here, and while you feel you're a bit stuck, this definitely isn't the worst place to be stuck. I mean, you have the beautiful pine trees on the mountains, and I'm sure the fields are green in the summer with crops and hay being grown. It might be a small consolation, but I think you're pretty lucky."

Preston turned his gaze to the fire, the bright reds and oranges reflecting in his eyes. "I guess I never thought about it like that. This is a beautiful place to be, even if there's snow for way too long every year."

Without thinking, Ashley slouched down, resting her head on his shoulder and leaning against his firm bicep. It felt perfect, but like so much in her life, it would only be that way for so long before things changed.

But she couldn't think about that at the moment. She was here for a short while, and he was her fake boyfriend. There was no promise of a future between them, no contract she needed to fulfill.

For those few moments before she shut her eyes, she felt the most peace she'd ever known in her lifetime. And for that, it was worth whatever small heartbreak she might feel once she left.

CHAPTER 15

*P*reston worked out in the cold, feeling the exhaustion from the past few days. He'd fallen asleep on the couch next to Ashley after fixing the toilet situation, and he'd never known such freedom as he did when he talked to her. But every time he thought about what he'd said about Walker and Lauren starting their relationship in the lodge, it made him cringe, hoping he hadn't made her think they would be anything more.

He didn't want to hold her back, didn't want her to stick around this small town for him, only to leave him after things got too boring for her adventurous spirit. But there was something about her that drew him in, and he couldn't get enough of her.

When he heard about the big auction and fundraiser for one of the young children in the community who'd been diagnosed with a rare form of cancer, he knew it would be a good way to get out and support along with the town while having a chance to be with Ashley.

He couldn't help but smile when she answered the phone later that afternoon.

"Did you hear about the fundraiser? I was wondering if I can swing by and pick you up?" Preston pawed at the damp ground outside with his boot, holding his breath as he waited for her answer.

"I did. Marsha can't come in until six tonight, but I'd love to go after that."

He pumped his fist in the air, grateful she couldn't see the action. "Great. I'll stop by around then."

It was hard not to keep smiling through the rest of his chores. Even mucking out the stalls, something he usually dished off to his younger brothers as often as possible, didn't bother him.

But then he remembered the milking. Seth and Tyler were already gone to who knew where. Maybe Adam would take over. He'd been helping by taking it over a few times over the past few weeks when Preston needed a night out and hadn't ever said much about it.

Walking into one of the outbuildings, Preston found his brother tinkering with the old tractor that hadn't worked in years.

"Are you free to milk tonight? I was thinking about taking Ashley to the fundraiser for the Berthold kid." Preston took off his gloves and blew on his fingers, causing the ends of them to tingle with the heat.

"Yep, I can do that. Better than trying to survive a crowd." Adam looked up and grinned at Preston, a smear of grease across one cheek.

Preston shook his head. "You and people. Most of them are good; I promise."

Adam stood and wiped his hands on an already soiled rag, shaking his head. "It's just easier to not have to come up with lame conversation. Or have them judge me for my career choice."

"Did you make a career choice?" Preston asked, his tone

giving away the teasing nature of the question.

His brother had been struggling the most since they'd lost their mother. He'd passed all his tests toward becoming a mechanic the year before, and while he went throughout the valley working on other farmers' equipment, Preston could tell he would rather be home at the farm, just fixing things instead of having to negotiate costs and invoices.

"Shut up," Adam said lazily. "What would the farmers do without me?" The statement wasn't boastful, not like most people would think.

Preston nodded. "You're right. There wouldn't be as much production in this valley if you weren't around. I'm going to head in and wash up, but thanks again for taking over for me. It makes me think I might not go completely crazy every time I see black and white together."

Walking out of the building, Preston had a lightness to his step and was grateful for his father and siblings. Each one of them brought a different dynamic to the family, but in the end, they made it work.

* * *

FINALLY FINDING a parking spot a few streets down from the gathering, Preston worked to parallel park his long truck, knowing it was going take a few tries to make it fit. But it was either that or make them walk even farther. He'd never seen so many cars in Afton, all of them congregating in the town hall for the fundraiser.

He walked next to Ashley on the sidewalk, trying to slow down as she stumbled in her heels once on the uneven cement.

"This is incredible. I didn't think there were this many people in the valley," she said, looking around at all the vehicles.

Preston nodded, rubbing his lips together against the cold. "We're a small town, but we come together when one of our own needs it. You should have seen the Christmas Ball last year. They organized a fundraiser for the Erickson family and raised enough money for them to have a nice Christmas and pay off several of the medical bills for the father. I heard they were able to purchase a home a few months ago, and his cancer is in remission."

He noted the look of delight in Ashley's eyes and couldn't help but be proud. Their valley knew how to band together when it counted.

Once inside the building, Preston turned and saw they were right next to three of the older ladies who'd each been badgering him to date for quite some time. He just wished he could explain that just because a woman was single, it didn't mean she would be the "perfect match" for him.

"Preston Burke, we haven't seen you in ages. How is your father doing?"

"Well enough," Preston said, shuffling his feet and glancing at the floor. It was the same old question that happened time and time again when he came to these events.

A warm hand enveloped one of his, and he looked over to see Ashley smiling at him. She squeezed once and then turned her gaze to the women.

"I'm Ashley Morgan. I've been in town for a few weeks and don't think I've met any of you."

Preston breathed out a sigh of relief as he watched the women's eyes take in the two of them holding hands and force smiles on their faces, each introducing herself in turn.

"We didn't know you were dating anyone, Preston," Thorna Lindley cooed. "I guess we'll just have to tell the ladies we wanted to set you up with that you're off the market…for now." Her last word seemed to anchor itself into his chest, causing him to need a deeper breath.

"It looks like they're getting started up there." Preston waved to the front of the room, grateful for some misdirection. "We should probably find our seats."

He tugged on Ashley's hand and moved them to an empty row of chairs about ten rows back. By the time everyone had settled in, most of the room was full.

"Thank you for that," he said, whispering in her ear. "I've avoided events like this for a while because of those three in particular."

Ashley gave a soft giggle and said, "Glad I could help."

He watched her full pink lips longer than he should have. But as they turned down, he frowned. "What's wrong?"

Shaking her head, Ashley leaned in closer, her lips tickling his ear as she said, "Look to your left."

Preston turned to see Jason and Quincy sitting in the chairs next to him. Well, if they were going to have to act like a couple for Preston, he might as well help her with her problem.

With a nod to say hello, Preston turned to look up at the front, his fingers interlocked with Ashley's and his thumb caressing the back of her hand. Jason shifted uncomfortably, and Preston had to work to keep his face passive, as if this was normal for the two of them.

Sure, they'd held hands in the lodge, but there was something electric about touching Ashley, as if she lit up nerves that hadn't been used in years with the touch of her skin against his.

"Thank you all for coming out to support the Berthold family," the mayor said through the microphone. "We have a lot to get through tonight, so we'll get right to it in about five minutes. If you haven't had a chance, there are some silent raffle prizes over here to the side which will be closing soon. The rest of the prizes will be auctioned live. After all the proceedings, there will be a light supper for all who want to stay."

The crowd buzzed, and Preston turned to look at Ashley when she pulled her hand from his as she stood.

"I'm going to go look at the silent auction items. Do you want to—" Ashley began but was interrupted.

"I'd love to go with you, Ashley," Quincy said, loud enough that several people turned to look in her direction. "It will be good to chat before the auction begins."

Preston stood. "I'd like to check them out as well." He slipped his hand back into Ashley's, feeling the warmth erupt through his arm. He didn't miss the look of disappointment on Quincy's face nor the look of gratitude on Ashley's.

As they walked away, he turned to see Jason still sitting in his seat, glancing at his phone. Ashley had been ready to marry that guy?

CHAPTER 16

They headed over to the long table set up with several items donated by the members of the community. Ashley's eyes filled with tears, making it difficult to see some of the items as she looked them over. What a great thing for a small town like this to help out a little four-year-old and his family.

"Look at this adorable sign, Ash," Quincy said. That helped clear away some of the emotion.

"I didn't know you were still in town, Q." Ashley stepped forward and picked up one of the large candles, breathing in the lovely pine scent.

Quincy's arm went to her hip, and she tapped Ashley on the shoulder. "What are you talking about? Jason and I have been enjoying the snow up in Jackson, and when we saw the sign about this fundraiser as we came back into town this afternoon, I told him we had to come."

Gritting her teeth, Ashley said, "Why are you not in Texas? Why are you waiting here?"

Quincy's expression changed, her jaw tightening. When she spoke, her volume lowered to the point that Preston didn't even turn. "If I leave, I won't know where you're off to next. We've got to fix this, Ash. We need our business to be running again."

As her mind went through a string of possible reasons why her cousin was so desperate for the blog to be up again, Ashley took one of the pens from the table and wrote a sum of money for one of the items on a small piece of paper, making sure to hide it from Quincy. She stuck it into the box and took a few steps to look at the prize Preston was toying with.

A hand gripped her upper arm, and Ashley turned to look at her cousin. "Don't just walk away from me, Ash. We've been besties since forever. Since when do you keep secrets from me?"

Ashley kept her voice even and low, wanting to get her point across. "Since you took my fiancé from me. What is so important that you need me to work on? You can post things just as well as I can."

Quincy worked her jaw back and forth. "We know what kind of engagement I get on posts. Our ads aren't making as much because people have already seen what we've got posted."

Pointing her finger at Quincy, Ashley said, "You're worried about money?"

"We just don't want to lose traction," Quincy said, tucking her hair behind her ear. "You know how the algorithms are on the internet and our social media. Quickstagram did another update, and we're going to need to start posting again." The entire time, Quincy wouldn't look Ashley in the eyes, and she knew that wasn't the entire story.

"I'll start posting again when I'm ready. For now, I'm taking a vacation, which is what normal people do around the holidays."

"Vacations are your job, Ash. I don't know what your

problem is. Take pictures of what you're doing now, at that lodge. Just start posting something."

"I think Jason just left," Preston said, pointing to the doors at the back of the room. "You might want to go catch him."

With a huff, Quincy turned on her heel and walked in the direction Jason had gone, giving Ashley a bit of relief.

"Thank you a hundred times. Who knew I could be so annoyed with my cousin?"

Preston shrugged, a grin on his face. "I think you've been more than civil to her. But it's strange she still keeps hanging around."

"Every time I just want to say I'm done with her and our business, I get a guilt trip from beyond the grave." She shook her head, chuckling at her own joke.

"What do you mean?" Preston side-eyed her as if she was losing it.

Ashley took a deep breath and gave him a half-smile. "My mom's mom, Grandma Shirley, was a Southern woman through and through. I loved her, but she knew how to play the cards so you felt guilty about something even if it wasn't your fault. I keep hearing her words that I need to give Q another chance or be patient with her."

"Isn't there a cap to the number of chances someone gets?" He smirked, and Ashley knew he was right. It was just going about it the right way that was going to be the tricky part.

The proceedings began, and Preston led her back to their seats. Ashley bid on a few things but was usually outbid in the live auctions. But when it came time for the results of the silent auction, her heart soared as she realized she'd won the prize she'd put in for.

"What did you win?" Preston asked as they walked out of the building and back to his truck.

Ashley held up the small clear package with a charm of a

deer on it. "Only the greatest thing ever. A deer charm!" She giggled as Preston made a face.

"Okay, but why that? Out of all the trips that were being auctioned off, you chose a small charm?"

"My mom had a really old charm bracelet from when she and my father first got married. She'd only collected two charms before she gave it to me in high school, and I've been collecting them from my travels ever since.

"And a deer will remind you of this trip?" His tone made her giggle again.

She pointed up as they walked under the horn arch stretching from one side of Main Street to the other. "How could I forget a place with all these horns? Jackson had a crazy amount too."

Preston let out a deep rumble and shook his head. "You are one of a kind, Ashley Morgan."

re you free Saturday night?

Ashley couldn't wipe the silly grin off as she stared at the words Preston had texted her a few minutes before. There was only a week left of her time as lodge manager, and there were already so many things tying her to this valley that the thought of moving on to the next place was scarier than ever before.

She'd been over to help with the milking twice, and she and Preston had gone into town for dinner another night since the fundraiser. Every time she was with him, she would laugh inwardly at the thought of ever having loved Jason. Her ex-fiancé would have been fine staying in and watching a movie or playing a video game for the rest of his life.

But Preston, he had a thirst for adventure she could see in his eyes. And the way she could have a full conversation with him, or when he opened her doors or held her hand and fireworks shot off inside her chest…She sighed.

I'm free. What did you have in mind? she replied, giggling to herself.

It didn't take long for his response to come in, and she

could picture him watching the screen, waiting for her answer.

Just make sure to dress warm. I want to take you somewhere.

At least she'd ordered a warm coat. It had already helped keep out some of the chill her several layers and jacket couldn't fight.

Two days later, she couldn't wait to see what the surprise would be. Marsha had taken over her shift a little early since Preston wanted to leave around three or three thirty in the afternoon. She swore the older woman was in on some secret, but she didn't dare ask for fear of spoiling whatever Preston had worked to put together.

The excitement of the whole thing nearly did her in as she'd never had a guy plan something special for her. The most romantic thing Jason had ever done was buy her some flowers from a road stand on one of their trips after she'd made several hints that she loved them.

When Preston showed up to the lodge, it took several moments for her to regain her breath. He wore what looked like a warm coat with a long t-shirt underneath that said something about the Utah State Aggies. And his jeans always seemed to fit him just right, making it so she had to avert her gaze to avoid alerting him that she was, in reality, checking him out.

As Marsha waved goodbye and winked at them, Ashley wondered why he'd gone to all the trouble of doing this. Maybe it was so Marsha could spread the word that they were, in fact, dating. But that thought took away some of the magic of the evening, so Ashley pushed it aside, hoping that wasn't the explanation.

When they climbed into his truck, Ashley saw a four-wheeler strapped to a trailer at the back. "Where are we going?" she asked, trying to be nonchalant.

"Just for a ride. I thought it would help you see the beauty of the Coldwater Creek Valley since you don't have much more time here." He paused and cleared his throat, glancing over at her nervously before looking back at the road. "Have you decided what you're going to do when Lauren and Walker come back?"

Shaking her head, she said, "There are so many options, but I've told Quincy we'll discuss everything tomorrow. She's actually been pretty good about leaving me alone for the past few days, but we can't go much longer without telling our readers what's going on and how we're going to move forward. She's posted a few pictures, but they haven't gotten the same traction we're used to."

He nodded, his expression revealing nothing. Part of her wanted him to beg her to stay, and she knew she just might accept at that point. This place was nearly magical, and it wasn't like she couldn't still go on trips every once in a while. But was that something he would want?

They'd driven for a few miles, chatting about their day, when he pulled into a large dirt parking lot at the base of some mountains. After unstrapping the four-wheeler, he tied a box to the back of it and told her to climb on.

They wound up a trail, Ashley sitting behind Preston with the wind blowing the amazing scent of his pine cologne to match the scenery, and she slid her arms around his waist, holding on despite the seat back she had to lean against. How could she have ever fallen for a guy like Jason when there was someone like Preston in the world?

It seemed like they rode for hours, but the sun still hadn't set quite yet. Her cheeks were frozen from the brisk air, but Preston's body seemed to shield the rest of her from freezing.

Once they made it to a large clearing, he pulled to a stop near a firepit and climbed off. Reaching up, he held her hand as she got down off the ATV.

"I can get down by myself, you know," she said with a smirk.

"I know. But I figured after we've been riding for so long that it might help to have someone to balance against. Even my legs are a little tingly." He grinned at her, and the thought crossed her mind to kiss him. He moved away, unstrapping the cooler and taking it over next to the firepit. He started digging out several pieces of trash out of the small ring of rocks and setting them to the side.

"Is there anything I can help you with?" Ashley asked, feeling useless at the moment.

"If you can find some dry wood, that would be good. I brought some, but not enough for the fire to keep for long."

Dry wood. She could do that. Being out in the woods wasn't something she was completely familiar with. Working in shops along a beachfront or even in a few fields, yes, but she'd never learned those survival skills for the wild that she was sure she'd need to use at some point in the future. Maybe this was a good start.

She made it to a grove of trees and picked up several thin branches that broke easily between her hands. Gathering a large armful, she brought them over and sat them next to the pit.

"These will be perfect fire starters, but we'll probably need some pieces a bit thicker." The way he said it was so nice, even though she got the intended meaning. *Nice try. Go look again.* "There is a small saw in the compartment on the four-wheeler if you feel comfortable using it."

Opening her mouth, she lifted a finger and said, "Let me go look again." Using a saw was another skill she'd never learned, and the thought of sawing off her thumb or fingers in the process caused her to shudder.

Walking a bit farther, she saw several trees downed and was sure she could find some bigger pieces of wood. There was a large tree branch at least the width of her leg. It was long and had several thicker branches attached to it. Working to drag it behind her, she made slow progress, yanking and pushing with her legs, hoping to get it back to the campsite.

Looking up, she realized she didn't recognize the area around her. Sure, there were plenty of pine trees, but she couldn't see her footprints on the ground, and there was no recognition of the area at all. She saw an opening that looked like a path and worked to pull the branch behind her, hoping the effort wasn't wasted.

Once she got there, it didn't open up to the clearing like she'd expected, and her stomach dropped as she wondered what she was going to do.

"Preston! Preston!" she called several times, hoping her voice would carry past the trees. She left the branch behind and wandered a bit farther, seeing the same green on either side of her. After a few more calls, she turned around, hoping one of the other areas were where she'd come through.

Her brain started buzzing, and she couldn't think straight as she tried to remember any little snippet of information she'd learned in her life about wilderness survival. Nothing would come except for the tightness in her chest and the spinning in her head.

"Preston! Can you hear me?" She tried to keep the panic from her voice, but it still wobbled near the end, and she had to focus on what to do rather than sit down and have a good cry.

She wandered for quite some time, trying different paths and hoping Preston would either hear her or come looking for her. At one point, the thought came to her that she needed to just sit down and wait, but the idea scared her. What if Preston didn't come looking or just couldn't find her?

She found a large rock and scooted herself onto the top of it, her legs dangling down. At first, she did everything she could to look at the positives: the wind wasn't as strong because of the thickness of the trees, and the sun hadn't completely gone down yet, allowing her to see some things.

After some time, though, her mind got the best of her, and she broke down, the tears streaming down her face. She'd never felt so scared and vulnerable, and the thought that a wild animal could attack her at any moment caused her to keep her sobs as quiet as possible.

She thought she heard some rustling and called out, "Preston?"

"Ashley!" The wind whipped by, making it hard to hear which direction she'd heard his voice come from, but at least she'd heard it.

The trees to her left rustled, and he came through them, the look on his face a mixture of anguish and terror. He walked right up to her and looked her over, holding her head between his hands and checking that she was okay.

"I'm so sorry. You're not hurt, are you?" He looked up at her eyes, wiping at the tears with his fingers. Without waiting for her answer, he wrapped his arms around her and gathered her to him. "I shouldn't have sent you for the wood alone. I'm so, so sorry."

"You're okay. I might have realized that trying to survive in the wild is not a good option for me." She smiled, hoping it would cheer him up just a bit. The fact that he'd shown up to rescue her had eased any anxiety she'd felt, and now she just wanted to get back to the four-wheeler. "How long have I been gone?"

"Over an hour. I couldn't remember which direction you'd gone the second time you went out, so I've been going out and doubling back to make sure you weren't back at the firepit already." He gave her another hug, and again,

Ashley felt safe, like he would do anything he could to protect her.

When he pulled back, he slipped his hand into her gloved one and guided her back to camp. It took them about fifteen minutes to get there, but at least she was with someone who had a better sense of direction than she did.

Preston added some wood to the pit and started the fire, pulling some packs of tin foil from the cooler. "I hope you like hobo dinners because that's what we're having." He gave her a half-grin, and Ashley laughed, the scene comical compared to the terror she'd felt minutes before.

"What's a hobo dinner?" she asked, feeling a little self-conscious that she had no idea.

"It goes by different names. Some people just call them tin-foil dinners. But it's basically ground beef with some good seasonings, potatoes, onions, and a scoop of condensed cream of mushroom soup." He moved some things around in the firepit and then set the two packages down on some white coals from the wood he'd put in. "Then we just let them cook for a bit and put on some ketchup or other sauce and dig in."

Ashley chuckled. This sounded like something a person who camped regularly knew about, which she did not.

Preston pulled a small saw out from under the seat of the four-wheeler and said, "I'm just going to go cut a bit more firewood, and then I'll be back. Just watch the fire, and I'll make sure I stay within hearing distance so you can call out if anything goes wrong."

"I appreciate that. I'd rather not have a near heart attack from fright again."

He gave her a small smile as if still berating himself for the whole situation. She could hear him sawing through the wood and took a deep breath. He was close, and she wasn't going to be lost forever. She kept repeating those words over and over again, hoping they would sink in enough to comfort her.

The memory of being at the state fair as a child and getting separated from her mom and dad crept into her mind, replaying with more clarity than she would have liked. Everywhere she'd looked, she couldn't find them. As a five-year-old, she could only remember her mom's first name, and since cell phones weren't commonplace yet, there weren't many ways to contact her.

Ashley remembered she'd decided to go back and stand in the spot she'd been in when she lost them, hoping they'd think to look there. It had seemed like an eternity in kid minutes, but they finally appeared, looking relieved and pulling her toward them. Was that what had prompted her to go sit down in one spot earlier? A memory of when she'd felt scared and then felt safe soon after?

Her mind mulled that thought over, trying to figure out why she'd felt so safe with Preston so many times before tonight. It wasn't like she'd been in danger in Coldwater Creek, but maybe it was because there was something about him that assured her he would do anything he could for her.

"Are you okay?" Preston asked, bringing several thick pieces of wood back and dropping them on the other side of the fire from where Ashley was sitting.

"I'm actually really good. Nothing to report scary-wise."

Preston looked a bit confused at first and then smiled at her. "That's always a good thing. Let me just get this wood in the fire, and I'll check on the dinners. They should be nearly done now."

Ashley watched as he moved with sure steps, amazed at all he knew. She'd grown up in the city, and there weren't a whole lot of skills needed to learn when traveling to the beaches of the world, except maybe CPR, which she'd used once on a little girl who'd gotten swept under a large wave and been unconscious for a bit. But those weren't the same dangers as the ones here, and she liked that Preston had that knowledge.

He pulled the packets of food onto a large rock and let them sit while he rummaged through the cooler. He handed her a paper plate with a plastic fork and knife and transferred one of the packets onto her plate.

"It's probably not the fanciest thing you've ever eaten. I hope you like it." He moved to plate his own food, adding a healthy dollop of ketchup to it.

"I haven't eaten at too many fancy places but this smells good. Thanks for giving me a chance in the real outdoors." She bit her lip, and her gaze dropped to the plate, feeling more vulnerable than she had in a while, this time more emotionally than physically.

What would she have done if he hadn't been able to find her? Would she have been fodder for a wild animal?

Shaking off those thoughts, she stabbed at some of the potatoes and stuck the bite into her mouth. She was safe and warm, in the protection of Preston. But she would definitely study up on survival skills once she made it back to the lodge.

*P*reston looked at Ashley, seeing the hesitation on her face. He could only imagine what she'd been going through as she waited for him to find her. He shouldn't have asked her to go out on her own, searching through unknown woods. Even though he knew she didn't have much experience with this kind of stuff, his brain had just treated her like she was Lauren and would know exactly what she was supposed to do to gather wood.

"Well, I hope I can make up for the scare you had earlier." He stuffed a bite of food into his mouth, forgetting to blow on it beforehand. He opened his mouth and tried to blow on it on his tongue, knowing he probably looked ridiculous. When it finally cooled enough for him to swallow, he did so, and the large piece moved slowly through his esophagus and into his stomach.

He needed to relax, to be grateful he'd found Ashley when he did. The sun was nearly down now, and while he could navigate the trails to get back to the truck with the help of the light on the four-wheeler, he'd forgotten a flashlight, which would have made a search for her in the dark much harder. He could have used the light on his phone if he needed to, but with the battery charge so low, it wouldn't have lasted long.

"Do you come up here often?" Ashley asked between bites of her food.

"Not so much anymore. We'd come up as a family sometimes on weekends in between milkings. Most of the time, my mom would bring us up and Dad would join us after. But it was always too short. That's the life of a dairy farmer."

Preston could feel Ashley's eyes on him, and he wondered what she was thinking.

"You don't like dairy farming much, do you?"

Sighing, he said, "I wish I could say I did, but in reality, I feel trapped. Like I can never fully relax because I have to get back at the right time for milking."

"What about tonight? Isn't it past time to milk the cows now?"

"Yes." Preston nodded. "But Adam said he'd take over for me tonight." He fiddled with the foil on his plate. "I just wish I'd had a say in the matter. It's hard to be living your dream and then have it stripped away without your say-so. I guess that's been the hardest part. I used to travel all over for the rodeo, and now it feels like I have to work out a whole schedule to get away for a few days."

Ashley scooted closer to him, a shiver moving through her body.

"Let me get you a blanket." Preston stood and grabbed one from the back of the four-wheeler, glad he'd remembered to pack one at the last minute. He walked back and wrapped it around her, staring at her perfect lips as she smiled a thank you.

There was a silence around them for a few minutes, and Ashley asked, "Is there a way to sell the farm, or at least lease out the cattle, so you can have an income every month but won't have to be on the clock every time?"

"I wish. I've probably gone over every scenario there is on how to get out of it. But if I give up, it only hurts my family. My two younger brothers are in high school or just starting college. They don't deserve to have no food because I'm being selfish."

She reached out and touched his arm with her hand, and even through all the layers he was wearing, he could feel a light tingle. He was falling hard, and he was going to be the one hurt in a few days when she up and left.

"I love it here," she said, staring up at the few stars coming out.

Preston looked up too, grateful for the clarity and relaxation he felt out here. "Me too."

She shivered again, and Preston wrapped his arm around her, pulling her closer. "Do you want to head back?"

"Not yet. I want to savor this time a little more."

"What is it you want out of life, Ashley Morgan?" Preston asked, his chin on top of her head. He breathed in the smell of coconut from her hair, fitting for the beach-loving girl. But could she stand to live in a valley surrounded by large mountains and piles of snow every winter? He couldn't think that far, or he'd only fool himself into hoping it would come true.

It was a long time before she answered, and part of him wanted to pull back and see if she'd fallen asleep.

"I'm not really sure yet. There are so many great positives about this place. I guess I just need to do a bit more soul-searching. Nothing like being in your late twenties and not having life figured out yet."

Preston smiled. "I don't think many people have anything figured out, let alone where their life is supposed to take them."

She leaned back, a touch of moisture in her eyes. Her gaze kept flicking to his lips and back up.

A punch of excitement filled his chest, and he moved in closer, joining his lips to hers. Every nerve ending seemed to be shooting off its own fireworks, and he could have sworn that a fire had started there.

He pulled back, looking into her eyes to see her reaction. She kept them closed and leaned against his shoulder, sighing loudly. He'd just have to take that as a good sign.

He needed to find a way to keep her in his life. How he was going to do that was going to be a challenge, but he had at least five days before his sister and Walker would be back. Hopefully, that would be enough time to come up with something.

CHAPTER 19

*A*shley turned off her alarm at least three times the next morning, deciding she'd rather keep dreaming about her evening with Preston than make herself completely presentable for the front desk.

It had ended nearly perfect, even though getting lost had been a major setback for her. The kiss they'd shared was electric, something she'd never felt kissing any other guy ever, which was saying something from some of the guys she'd met in exotic locations. Kissing Jason now seemed like kissing a dead fish—no passion and no sparks whatsoever. The more she hung out with Preston, the more she realized just how lucky she was to avoid that whole disaster. Quincy could have him.

She managed to make it downstairs in time to take over for the night manager. With everything quiet, she sat down and put a little mascara on, knowing she didn't want to scare away any customers with her tired look.

The morning flew by with several people checking out and the reports coming in from the maids and the breakfast. But by the time noon hit, it seemed the lodge was completely dead. The restaurant didn't open on Sundays, and with most guests already checked out, it was going to be a slow afternoon, except for her impending discussion with Quincy. What time that would happen, she wasn't yet sure, but she hoped it would be after her shift.

The door opened around four, and Ashley looked up to see Quincy with Jason trailing behind her.

"Oh good, you're here. It seems like every time I've tried to find you lately, you've been with that farmer boy. Are you really dating him?" The sneer in her voice made Ashley's defenses rise and she took a breath, trying to calm herself before exploding.

"Yes, we've been dating, and I've learned quite a bit since. But we might as well get started with our discussion, Quincy." It was better to get to the heart of the matter rather than try to argue over something Ashley didn't care to worry about.

Seeing Jason over her cousin's shoulder, a sense of relief rushed over Ashley, and the hurt and betrayal she'd felt just a few weeks before dissipated. Even if her future wasn't supposed to be with Preston, she knew now what qualities she wanted in a future partner.

"I doubt you've checked your email in a while, but we've received a request from one of the biggest resorts in Mexico." Quincy took a seat in the empty chair next to Ashley, leaving Jason to lean against the wall, silent and looking bored.

Ashley sighed. "When do they want us to be there?"

"By the end of the week for at least two weeks. They're hoping to get a good push before Thanksgiving so they can sell out for the Christmas holiday." Quincy paused for a moment, her eyes flicking over Ashley's appearance. "This is a big payday, Ash. We can't just turn it down."

"We should probably discuss how we're going to do things now before we start taking on more jobs, Q." Ashley glanced at the small calendar on the desk, seeing that the trip would take them through Thanksgiving. She'd never been one for worrying about where she'd be for a holiday, but this was the first time she wished she would be staying in Cold-water Creek. If they did accept the job, she'd need to give Preston a heads-up early on so he wouldn't be expecting her.

Frowning, Quincy folded her arms across her chest and leaned back in the seat. "What are you talking about? You can't just give up on the business, Ash. Most of the people who reach out to us do so because of you. Without you, the business falls flat."

Ashley couldn't help the feeling of satisfaction that flowed through her. While Quincy was another writer and owner of the company, she was more into the behind-the-scenes of the website, setting up the places and getting everything orga-nized for trips. She was right about things not working as smoothly without Ashley.

"Okay, then. I want more time in between trips." Ashley matched her cousin's pose, narrowing her eyes as if in some sort of showdown challenge.

"What are you talking about? You get to tour some of the greatest places in the world on a weekly or monthly basis. What's not to love about that?"

Ashley raised her eyebrows and leaned forward. "We're not getting any younger, Q, and at some point, I want to settle down and raise a family. That's not the easiest thing to do when I'm jet-setting to foreign destinations every other day. Obviously, when I lost a fiancé because I was 'gone so much,' as you put it. Maybe something you should consider as well." Ashley's gaze flicked to Jason and rolled back to Quincy. "I just need a bigger break in between. If the money isn't coming in as much, then it's not the end of the world."

Jason shifted uneasily, and red covered Quincy's features. If she were a cartoon character, there would've been air shooting out her ears at that point. "What do you mean, 'it's not the end of the world'? That money affects all of us, not just you."

"I didn't mean it that way," Ashley said, ready to be done with the conversation. "I'm just saying I need some more time between bookings. We can find other ways to make up the revenue using ads or more blog posts, but let's use our heads."

Quincy stood abruptly, looking like she was about to throw a temper tantrum. "Of course, because no one is as smart as Miss Ashley Morgan."

She turned to walk out, and Ashley wasn't sure if she should run after her or stay seated. Over the course of their business partnership, Ashley had always been the one mending fences and making sure the waters were calm between them, but she wasn't feeling that at the moment.

"I'll do the trip to Mexico, only if you agree to more time between trips," Ashley called after her.

She could barely see above the tall desk of the lodge, and Quincy stopped just inside the door. All that could be seen over the top were her eyes, narrowed. Ashley could imagine her pinched lips looking as though she'd just bitten into a lemon, but she wasn't about to be moved on this. If there was one thing she'd learned in her short tenure in Coldwater Creek, it was that there was so much more to see than just dollar signs.

Quincy moved out the door, and Ashley turned back to her phone to check on something she had been doing before she was interrupted.

"She's sorry, you know." Ashley jumped at Jason's voice, having forgotten he was still there.

"Sorry about what?" Ashley asked, the curiosity pulling the question out of her.

Jason moved forward and took the seat Quincy had just

vacated. "About how things ended between the two of us. I'm sorry too, Ash. I just think I'm a better match for her than we would have been together."

"I'm not arguing with you on that. I'm just looking for a little leeway in my life, a chance to experience things that don't have to be captured on camera and then shared with the world."

His jaw worked back and forth a few times, and he glanced toward the door before speaking. "We're getting married right before Christmas. Quincy secured a venue, and the wedding planner has agreed to do it for promotion. We're also under contract to sell some of the photos to one of the major publications."

Ashley sat back, feeling as if he'd just blown up her world and held her under water for too long. "Wait, what? You're getting married in December? We just broke up a month ago." Her jaw dropped open as she tried to work through all he'd said. Of course, Quincy would work every angle of this. It was a way to cut Ashley out of at least one way of making money.

"She's been trying to get up the courage to ask you to be her bridesmaid."

"Then why are you the one telling me?" Ashley stood, needing a bottle of water or something to quench the desert in her mouth.

"I just wanted you to be prepared for it. I know this has all been a whirlwind, but you do much better when you've been given fair warning." Jason seemed to see through her.

Ashley paused before continuing into the next room. She'd been okay with her cousin taking her ex-fiancé when the day began, but now that Quincy was taking her dream of getting married at Christmas and using it as a photo op? That didn't sit well.

And to top it off, she'd have to stand by and watch it all

happen. They'd made a pact that they would be each other's maid of honor, but the thought now brought a bitter taste to her tongue. She'd have to find some loophole that got her out of it. Maybe she'd set up a work trip on her own with the excuse that she couldn't turn it down. But being there was expected by so many people, even if the bride had been switched out. But she couldn't think about that now.

Even as she thought about it, her grandmother's words rang through her head, *Blood is thicker than water, child. Sometimes we have to suffer through the discomfort of situations for the happiness of our family.*

Quincy's wedding was the last thing she wanted to do at Christmas. She'd only heard about the amount of snow that came into Coldwater Creek Valley, but she'd found herself wanting to experience it in all aspects, including Christmastime. She didn't want to have to traipse off to whatever island Q had chosen for the venue and be bossed around by her cousin.

Pulling a soda from the refrigerator in the break room, Ashley took a long swig, the bubbles burning her throat as they went down. It was something she needed, though, a physical pain taking over her more immediate emotional one.

She heard the bells ring above the front door and moved back out to see who it was, hoping it wasn't Quincy returning to continue their argument. When she got to the front, it was empty, and Jason was walking to the car.

Breathing a sigh of relief, she sat back in her seat, wondering what to do with her life. She wanted to call Preston and tell him all about it, but that sliver of hope she saw in his eyes every time he asked about her future plans held her back. She couldn't promise him she'd stay in Coldwater Creek, no matter how much she wanted to right then.

And he couldn't just pack up and leave at a moment's notice like she'd gotten used to.

An ache started in her chest and seemed to move deeper by the minute, telling her that whatever decision she made, she would lose on some front.

CHAPTER 20

*P*reston had been on cloud nine all day, thinking about the night before. He'd been up most of the night, hoping to figure out some way that he and Ashley could make a relationship work, but with the dairy and his father's physical therapy appointments, it just seemed next to impossible.

He'd gotten busy with milking that evening, but the next morning, he called Ashley, hoping to set up something for later that evening. Lauren had sent him some pictures of their trip, and he yearned to be escaping now, wanting to be adventuring on hikes and seeing different places with Ashley.

Ashley didn't pick up, and he chalked it up to a busy morning at the lodge. He'd been there early on some mornings, and at just the right time, there could be a line of people waiting to check in to their rooms. Probably not so much on a Monday morning, but he gave her the benefit of the doubt.

He texted her later, hoping to hear something back with enough time to ask Adam to take over for him that night in the milking barn.

I'm so sorry. Things are really busy here tonight, and Marsha called in sick. I don't think I can make it, she replied.

Preston wasn't sure why he felt so disappointed, because this was the first time she'd turned him down, and it was for valid reasons, not just because she didn't want to hang out with him. But he'd been hoping to continue chatting, to get to know her more and hopefully figure out how they could have a real relationship instead of one that had all the town gossips leaving him alone when it came to dating.

No problem. We can try tomorrow.

He waited for a quick response, but nothing came through for minutes. He moved back into the living room, trying to relax a bit. The snow had begun to fall that morning, and he still felt like every part of him was frozen.

His father scooted into the room, and Preston hopped over to help him sit in his chair. "Looks like winter is coming in early."

"Yep," Preston said, taking a seat on the couch. "It's just as cold as ever out there."

"Adam said things are going smoothly out there. All the cows are milking well?" His father's lips worked to get the words out, sometimes slurring them together with the paralyzed side.

Nodding, Preston said, "For the most part. The vet should be by to preg-check several of the cows tomorrow so we can get a count for how many we'll have come spring."

"You're doing a good job, Preston. Your mother would be proud." His father tried to smile, the one side of his face drooping a bit more than normal.

"Are you feeling okay today, Dad? You look really pale." Preston leaned in, trying to remember what his dad had looked like the day before, hoping he was just seeing things.

His father smiled wider. "I'm feeling good today. Just needed a bit more rest than normal, but I'm still here." He took in a ragged breath before asking a question that threw Preston off guard. "I've heard that you've started dating someone. A new girl to Coldwater Creek?"

It took several seconds for Preston to figure out what to say to that. "Um, well, we've gone on a few dates so far." That was the truth. He hated to lie to his father.

"Do you like this girl?"

"Yeah, I do. In some ways, she reminds me of Mom. Full of spunk and adventure." Preston looked down at his hands, hoping he didn't convey how much he wanted to be out there adventuring right now.

"That does sound like your mother. She was always working to find something to take you kids to, whether it was overnight camping or exploring different parts of the valley. I think she secretly loved it when you were in the rodeo so she could travel to different states."

"Yeah, those were some good times." Times when she was healthy and not cancer-ridden.

His father reached out with his good hand and patted Preston's hand. "She's probably worth the adventure, then, right?"

Not wanting to divulge the entire mixed-up scenario that was now his life, Preston nodded. He wasn't sure how to make it all work, but he'd give it a try. If she'd let him see her, that is.

"Will she be staying in Coldwater Creek?"

"I'm not sure, but I doubt it would be long-term if she did. She has a business in travel and is asked by resorts to stay at their places and recommend them to her blog readers and followers. It would be hard to change a life of travel to stay in one place for long." And what would happen if he asked her to stay? Would she resent him because of the boredom he himself was already feeling?

His father nodded, his usual sign that he was thinking

about something. "A traveling girl, huh? Sounds a lot like you, son. I wish I could do something to change your circumstances so you could have the chance to pursue her further." The sadness that spread across his father's face made a hard knot of guilt form in Preston's throat.

"I don't blame you, Dad. You've been at the head of this family for nearly four decades, and it's not bad to have your kids help you out."

"I'm your father," he said, his voice quivering a bit. "I'm supposed to be able to take care of you until I die, and here I am, useless in so many things."

Kneeling on the floor, Preston took his father's hand in his. "Dad, we're going to be fine. If she wants to stay, she'll stay. If not, then she isn't worth my time worrying about. I'm here, and I'll make sure this family doesn't go without."

His father's eyes were hooded, but two tears slid down his cheeks, making it difficult for Preston to keep his own emotions under control. "Your mother would be right proud of the man you've become. I just hope everyone can see how much you've sacrificed to take care of your family. If there's ever a way to make it easier for you, I'll make that decision, hard or not."

The landline rang, and Preston stood, sniffing a bit. He answered the call and brought the cordless remote to his father so he could talk with one of his friends down the road.

Heading out to the mudroom, Preston donned his rubber boots and thick coat, knowing a little physical exertion would do him some good.

He couldn't make Ashley's decision for her, but he hoped she felt the connection to him that he felt toward her. Because having her by his side would make the long, dull days much more meaningful.

CHAPTER 21

The days passed quickly, and Ashley hadn't seen Preston once since their kiss. He'd tried to make plans several times, but as much as she wished she could see him, she knew it would make it that much harder to move on when Lauren and Walker returned.

When Walker's old beat-up truck pulled back into the drive of the lodge, Ashley wasn't sure if she'd be able to control her emotions. It wasn't like anything totally life-changing had happened in the past three weeks, but the fact that she'd figured out so much about herself in that time seemed as likely as getting struck by lightning. She'd come so far, and a good part of the credit was due to Preston.

Walking in the door, Lauren was all smiles, heading directly to Ashley and pulling her into a rib-crushing hug. "I can't begin to thank you for giving us this opportunity to venture out and have a vacation together. It was something we definitely needed, without all the stress of the lodge. Did everything go okay?"

Ashley nodded, trying to keep her voice even. "Yeah, everything went smoothly. You've got a great staff here, and they were awesome about keeping me updated on everything. And I fell in love with Coldwater Creek." Her eyes moved to something on the other wall as she thought about Preston. Was she in love with him too? There were so many strong feelings for the man who made her feel safe and listened to what she had to say, letting her have her opinions.

As if knowing where her thoughts had gone, Lauren asked, "Did Preston check in on you?"

Ashley's eyes snapped up, and she tried to think of something to say. "Yes, he did a great job of making me feel welcome. He even took me up on the trail he said your mom and dad used to take you all for quick trips."

Lauren's mouth dropped open, and her eyes went wide. "He took you up there? I don't think he's ever taken anyone there."

As her cheeks heated, Ashley raised her hands to hide them, hoping Lauren wouldn't guess that they'd shared their first and only kiss up there.

"Well, I hope you plan to stick around for a bit longer. We can always use some more fun younger people in town. Most people like to move away as soon as high school is over."

Walker came in and chuckled. "Yeah, but there are a lucky few who make it back here and remember how great the valley can be." He leaned forward and kissed Lauren on the lips. It was light and quick, but a strange bit of envy ran through Ashley that she didn't have that opportunity. Then again, she'd been the one pushing Preston away for the past few days.

"I actually head out tomorrow. We got asked to review a big event at one of the resorts in Mexico, so I'll be on a plane sooner than I want to." She could feel the truth of that statement sink deeper and deeper, making her wonder if continuing with the website was something she really should be doing. If she had someone at her side, someone to share the experiences with, someone like Preston, her life would be the complete package of happiness.

Lauren frowned. "Oh no, I'm so sorry. What if we invite you to our Christmas party? It's Christmas Eve, and we have a bunch of fun together here at the lodge. Would you make room to come back for that? We'd love to see you again and thank you for all you did to help us out during this time."

Smiling wide for the first time in a few days, Ashley nodded. "I would love that." The idea of coming back was like a breath of fresh air, one she needed if she was going to survive a two-week trip to a Mexican resort with her cousin.

Ducking behind the desk, Lauren started clicking things on the computer and then said, "We agreed on six thousand for your time here, right?"

Ashley hadn't even thought about being paid for her time at the lodge, and now it seemed like she'd be robbing them if she took the money. "No charge. Think of it as a really late wedding present from me to you."

"No, no, no," Lauren began, waving her finger at Ashley. "With all you did to help us, you at least need to be compensated."

"I promise, Lauren, I've been overpaid in so many other ways that I can't take your money. This place helped give me the perspective I need for life. But I will take you up on coming to stay for Christmas. I'll let my cousin know so she can put it on our calendar." Ashley hoped it would be the same time Quincy and Jason were getting married, if that was actually going to happen. That would be a viable excuse to miss the wedding. She was surprised Q hadn't told her the date or even where the wedding was happening yet.

"Perfect!"

They finished up their conversation, and Ashley moved back up to her room where she flopped on the bed. She'd spent several months in a few places and had never felt so connected as she did to Coldwater Creek. If only she could box it up and bring it along with her on her travels.

Just wanted to say I've missed talking to you. I hope you're good.

A mixture of sadness and regret washed over Ashley as she read Preston's words. How had she fallen for him already? He was definitely the reason she didn't want to leave, but what was she going to do for a job here? There were probably other positions out there, but she also owed it to her readers to give them some of the content they'd missed out on in the past five weeks. At least until she came to a final conclusion.

I've missed you too.

It was all she could send, even though she wanted to pour her heart out to him through text. Their lives were so different, and as much as Preston wanted to travel, she knew taking care of his family was the biggest priority. How could she ask him to give that up to join her on her adventures?

She must have fallen asleep because when she awoke, it was dark out and her phone said it was nearly seven. Taking the stairs down to the restaurant, she asked the hostess for a table for one, knowing she needed to get something in her soon. She hadn't eaten lunch and didn't have enough snacks in her room to hold her over until the next morning.

Before she'd been seated, a familiar voice came from behind her. "You're still alive."

Turning, she saw Preston standing there, one hand stuffed into his pants pocket and the other holding a single white rose.

"What are you doing here?" she asked, accepting the rose from him. "And how did you know that white roses are my favorite?"

"I wanted to see you," he began, his expression turning

sheepish when he continued with the next part, "and I may have done a little research about your favorite flower."

Ashley racked her brain, trying to figure out where she'd mentioned they were her favorite. Not in any of their conversations. Maybe on the blog?

"Well, thank you for it. This is beautiful." She held the flower to her nose and breathed in the scent, the whole scene almost out of a fairy tale.

"May I join you for dinner?" Preston asked.

Ashley nodded. She was going to be in trouble when she had to leave in the morning, but she couldn't help wanting one more night to hang out with him. "I fell asleep after Lauren and Walker got back, so I'm not very dressed up. I hope you don't mind."

"I think you look great." He moved forward, tucking a piece of hair behind her ear, causing her breath to hitch in her chest. She kept glancing at his lips, wondering what it would be like to kiss him again, more of a farewell kiss than anything.

The hostess came back and said, "Your table is ready."

There was already another setting on the other side of Ashley's, and Preston held her chair out for her to sit down first before moving to his own.

He folded his hands together on the table and asked, "So now that you're done here, what's next for you?"

Ashley saw the same hesitation as the other times he'd asked her, but this time, it seemed more urgent, as if he knew there weren't many days left to see each other.

"Well, I fly to Mexico tomorrow morning." She hadn't meant to be so blunt, but she knew that if she didn't tell him now, she'd avoid it and really hurt him when he found out she was gone the next day.

His expression fell, and his gaze went to his hands twisting the wrapper from a straw around his fingers. "That's great. Sounds like the perfect place to be with the cold weather about to hit." His voice was calm, measured, and it nearly broke her heart to hear him speak like that.

She nodded. "Quincy booked it a few days ago. I'm just hoping it's a quick trip." Looking up at Preston, she said, "Lauren invited me here for Christmas."

His gaze shot up, and the smile that crossed his face made her heart melt. At least she knew he had some feelings for her, maybe not to the extent that she did for him, but some were better than none at all.

"And?"

"And I'm going to do everything I can to come. I would love to spend Christmas here, to see what this town is like covered in snow, even though we've had small flurries of it until now."

Preston's smile faded a bit, causing him to look overly serious. "Do you care if I call or text you while you're gone?"

A quick zing of excitement shot through her. "I would love that, but I might not have reception while we're in Mexico. I'll respond as soon as I can once I'm back in the states."

"A traveling girl doesn't have a phone that can work internationally? That sounds like a bad business move to me," Preston said, grinning wide.

"Well, I need to get a new phone and don't have time to do that before I leave for the trip. My screen got smashed yesterday, and the phone store here in town doesn't have phones with that capability."

They chatted for a while, and after dinner, Ashley was a bit nervous about what to do. Should she hug him so she could trap the scent of him into her memory for the next few weeks? Or did she shake his hand and tell him she'd see him when she saw him?

He made the decision for her, pulling her to him at the

staircase that led up to her room in the lodge. "Did I hear right that Quincy and Jason are getting married in a few weeks?"

She pulled back, trying to read his expression. "Jason told me that, but I haven't seen anything in the media about it, so I thought it was just some strange dream I was having."

Preston frowned, his eyebrows combining to make a long blond line. "Does it still hurt that they betrayed you?"

"No," Ashley said, shaking her head. "It's just that it's so fast, and that's when Jason and I were supposed to get married. I've always loved the idea of a winter wedding, and it's just a little odd that they're getting married so quickly. Where did you hear about it?"

"Posted on your business Quickstagram account. Looks like there are a lot of confused followers wondering if someone made a mistake and put Quincy's name instead of yours."

Ashley couldn't help but laugh. So he had been researching on her social media and blog. "I'm sure. I haven't been on there in forever, but I never posted anything about us breaking up. Just one more thing to smooth over."

They hugged again and said good night, and even though she knew she shouldn't be, she felt disappointed that he hadn't tried to kiss her again. Maybe she should have leaned in, but would that have just made things more complicated?

Back in her room, she packed up the things she wasn't going to need in the morning before she drove back to Jackson to catch her flight out.

"I'll be back for Christmas," she kept telling herself to keep the bay of tears from spilling out. "Just a few weeks away, and you'll see him again."

CHAPTER 22

Two weeks later, Preston drove to the lodge to have lunch with Lauren and Walker. They had been two of the longest weeks of his life, knowing he wouldn't be able to talk to Ashley. He just wished he'd said how he felt about her before she left for Mexico. He still didn't know if she felt the same, but there had to be some feelings reciprocated. Or was he just trying to kid himself?

"You look rough, brother. What's wrong with you?" Lauren asked, greeting him as he walked through the front door of the lodge.

"I don't know. I'm an idiot." He rubbed his hands over his face, feeling like he was stuck doing something he could never get out of. His life.

Lauren cocked her hip to the side and sat a hand on it, giving him that bored expression she was so good at. "Well, I could have told you that. Dad said you've been moody the past couple weeks, and I think you miss a woman by the name of Ashley."

"So what if I do? It's not like there's any future for the two of us. I'm stuck here with the cows and the farm, and she's out traveling and seeing the world."

"Is it her you miss or just getting out of this town?" Lauren raised her eyebrows, and Preston felt his defenses rise.

"I miss her, okay. I'd be fine on the farm if she were by my side. I just don't want to tie her down when she has the freedom to be out running her business." Preston slumped down onto a chair in the nearly empty dining room. The advantage of getting up early to milk the cows was that he usually needed lunch much earlier than the rest of the world.

Lauren took a seat next to him, and when Walker joined them, Lauren filled him in. Preston was grateful for that as he didn't want to rehash everything a million times.

"So, what are you going to do?" Walker asked, taking a sip of ice water from the glass in front of him.

"I don't know," Preston said, throwing his hands into the air in frustration. He leaned back against the chairback. "I've been watching her website and social media like an addict, hoping for some hint as to when she'll be back stateside."

"You could always message her on her different accounts," Lauren offered. "Tell her how you feel and see what she thinks."

Preston shook his head. "I don't want her nosy cousin to see our conversation. Ashley doesn't always have control over the social media."

"It's worth a shot. Maybe the cousin is happy now that she's getting married." Walker shrugged, looking like he was ready for the conversation to change. He'd never been good with relationships that ended with someone leaving another person, having gone through it himself, and Preston could see the discomfort now.

Preston nodded. "Okay, I'll do that. It's not as romantic as telling her I'm head over heels in love with her in person, but because I got so tongue-tied the last time I saw her, it will have to do until I can see her again."

They made it through lunch, but Preston didn't add much, trying to decide the best wording to send in a message to Ashley. He'd do it when he got home, and if he was lucky, he'd have her response within the next day.

Twenty-four hours later, Preston felt like a zombie who hadn't slept much, waking up every so often to check his messages. He was acting like a lovesick puppy, and he was okay with it. Thanksgiving had been the week before, and he wished he'd asked her when she would be back in the States before she'd left Coldwater Creek.

He worked to get himself going, trying to convince himself that maybe it had only been an infatuation on her end.

CHAPTER 23

*I*t had also been a long couple of weeks for Ashley. While she'd enjoyed her time in Mexico, she was ready to be back in the States, just to have a regular American cheeseburger. She also wanted the chance to talk to Preston, hoping they'd be able to talk about how much she'd missed him.

She'd spent most of the time at La Riviera Grand Resort, thinking about him and how much fun it would be to have him around, enjoying the sand and all the events the place had to offer. Instead, she had to watch Quincy and Jason talk endlessly about their wedding preparations to everyone they encountered. How her cousin had gotten the homebody to travel once again was beyond her, but that was beside the point.

There *had* been several moments where Ashley was able to escape, like going on a ziplining trip by herself since Quincy and Jason were both terrified of heights. She'd also taken a hike with a good-sized tour group, where she was amazed by the beauty.

Thanksgiving wasn't the traditional meal of turkey and

potatoes either. The resort had a banquet set out for its American tourists, filled with entrees from around the world, and although it was just as good as any other meal, Ashley still longed to be back in Coldwater Creek with a handsome dairy farmer.

Once they landed back in Texas, Ashley made her way to the phone store, knowing she needed to get her phone fixed in the hopes that she'd be able to talk to Preston sooner. She called him, with no answer, then dialed her mother.

"Hey, Mom. How have you been?"

"Much better now that I finally get to hear from you. It's been so long, honey. Where have you been traveling lately?" Her mother's voice was somewhat soothing for her, helping her take her mind off talking to Preston for a few moments.

"I was in Wyoming for about five weeks and just got back into the States from Mexico."

"A month, huh? I thought the beach was more your style."

Leave it to her mother to cut right to how she was feeling about things. "I did too, but after breaking up with Jason, I thought I'd try something different, and I'm so glad I did. But I can't get Q and Jason to leave me alone now."

"Are you going to the wedding?"

"I've gone back and forth over it the past few weeks, and I don't know. You remember how close we were and that stupid pact we made so long ago. Q has a dress fitting for us in a couple hours, and I'm not sure I can go through with it. I just keep having Grandma Shirley's words running through my head that it's a family event and we support family."

"I get that. My mother's voice runs through my own head more than I want it to, and it's usually with that special side of guilt she always knew how to serve, whether it was to family or friends." There was a pause on the other line, and then her mother said, "Do you still love Jason?"

"No." The word came out faster than Ashley had expected.

"How do you feel toward Q now? I know it's hard because of the betrayal, but you survived two weeks with her in Mexico. Would you be able to live your life knowing you didn't go to the wedding?"

"That's a good question. One I'll have to think about. I've got to run, Mom, but I'll make sure to call in a couple of days."

"You'd better. I don't worry as much when I know where you are."

Ashley said goodbye and hung up the phone, feeling only slightly better. Her relationship with her mother was like a long-time friend who she could catch up with and not have any hurt feelings about the length of time in between. Her mother was busy enough with Ashley's stepfather's family, but it was nice to know she had some support. At least she wasn't the only one in the family who kept hearing her grandmother's voice.

Maybe to be present would be enough, and then she could sever ties with the two of them after the wedding. There wouldn't be many big events she'd have to "support" her cousin through after a wedding, and after the trip to Mexico, it was clear their business needed to change, whether it was Ashley leaving or Quincy.

She didn't have much time after their phone call, as Quincy had scheduled several appointments to get fittings done for her wedding dress and Ashley's maid of honor dress.

By the time the day was through, she was ready to be alone, away from the bossiness of her cousin who was acting like she was the princess who'd been shunned her entire life.

Ashley tried calling Preston, hoping to hear his voice after so long, but it went to voicemail.

"Hey, Preston. This is Ashley Morgan. I'm so sorry it's been so long, but I just made it to Texas this morning, and I've been running wedding errands all day with Quincy. Um, they're going to have the wedding here in Texas, the same place I'd reserved for my supposed-to-be wedding." She took a quick breath and then said, "Sorry, I'm rambling. Call me, will you? I've missed our chats."

She hung up the phone and continued to stare at the screen. There was only one place she wanted to be right then, and it was in Coldwater Creek.

The next few days felt like more than she could handle, and Quincy seemed to be going all bridezilla on the entire operation. They were two days away from the nuptials, and the dread seemed to grow with each passing hour for Ashley. She'd have to smile and pretend all was normal to all the guests, most of whom would have been there for her wedding.

She'd called and texted Preston a few times, wondering why he hadn't called yet. Each time, she built a renewed hope that he would contact her, but as the day would wane, she realized he wasn't going to call. Had she been the only one to think their time together was magical? That the kiss they'd shared on the mountain was like fireworks at Disneyland?

He'd been the one to ask her to stay in touch, and now he wasn't answering. She just hoped something hadn't happened at home to his family. His father's health hadn't been the best, but she'd never officially met him, so she wasn't sure if it was deathbed serious or just the after-effects of the stroke.

She texted him one more time, knowing she'd have to let go completely if he didn't answer.

I hope all is well with you and your family. Let me know if you need to talk about anything.

It was vague and showed as much affection as if they

were just friends, but she wasn't sure what to do at this point. Should she even show up to Christmas with his family in a week if he wasn't talking to her?

"Are you still trying to get ahold of farmer boy?" Quincy asked with a sneer, coming up behind her.

"Maybe." Ashley was about ready to be done with her cousin and the attitude she'd put up with over the past few weeks, but at this point, she didn't know what she'd do if she never heard from Preston again. She'd concocted several fantasies about a future together, and she'd nearly convinced herself that it was in the small Wyoming town where she should settle down.

"I thought you'd give up after you hadn't heard from him. You're so much better than a dairy farmer's wife." Quincy glanced in the mirror on the wall in the living room of the apartment they'd shared for a few years.

Ashley couldn't contain her fury any longer and shook her head. "I don't know what your deal is, but I'm old enough to decide what I want and don't want in life. You're getting your fairytale wedding with all the pictures in the world. Why do you have to keep making remarks like that? Are you not actually happy about marrying Jason?" Looking at her hands, Ashley realized they'd been flailing throughout her speech, and she dropped them down at her sides, taking in a deep breath so she could control anything that came next.

Quincy gave her the well-practiced expression of shock and took a seat. "I'm sorry, Ashley. I guess I just wanted us to be back to normal, back to the way we were when we started our travel-review company. But if you decide to settle down in Coldwater Creek, where does that leave our friendship and, more importantly, our business?"

"Back to normal? It can never be normal between us now, Q. After everything you've pulled, all the backstabbing and manipulating, I don't trust you. I'm not sure what's in my future, but don't you think I deserve to figure that out on my own? Maybe things with Preston won't work out because of his not being able to leave the farm often, but what if they do? Am I not allowed the same chance at happiness that you've been trying to steal from me this whole time?" Ashley's chest rose and fell, trying to replace the amount of air she'd expelled in the few sentences.

Quincy had a curious look like she was trying to apologize for something. "You might want to see this, then." She pulled out her phone and tapped several times on the screen before holding it out for Ashley to see.

"What is this?" Ashley asked, bridging the distance between them and taking the phone from her cousin.

Quincy bit her bottom lip for a few seconds and said, "It's a message from Preston. One he sent while we were still in Mexico. I deleted it after screenshotting that picture."

Glaring at her cousin, she felt the irritation swell in her chest. "You deleted one of my private messages before I could read it?"

"I just couldn't have you leaving already. I saw it during the second week of our trip when I was checking all of our social media accounts, and there was just so much riding on that trip. I didn't want you to disappear and run back to him." Quincy opened her mouth as if to say more, but Ashley held up a finger.

"Let me read it."

She clicked on the picture to allow for the type to be a little bigger on the small screen.

Ashley,

I know we've only known each other for a few weeks, but I feel more alive in the time I've spent with you than I ever have before. I didn't think I could even hope to have a relationship with being so tied to the farm, but after meeting you, I've been hoping to find a way to do that. With you.

I don't know if you've felt the same sparks I have every time we've been together, but just know that I care for you. I like you. I might even feel more than that. I know I should have told you all this before you left, but I couldn't find the right words to say it.

I'll wait to hear from you in the next few days. I hope you had a great trip, and don't forget that someone in Coldwater Creek is thinking about you.

-P

Tears were streaming down Ashley's face, and she wiped them away as she read it all over again and forwarded it to her phone. This had been from ten days ago. What must he be thinking of her now?

"I can't believe you kept this from me. I haven't done anything to get in the way of your happiness, even though you basically took over my wedding for me. Not that I regret that now, but the way you've treated me, the way you've manipulated me into doing things just so you could have your cushy paycheck from the resorts..." Ashley looked around the room and then back at her cousin. "I'm done. I can't do this anymore. You can tell people what you want, but I'm not going to stick around because you're worried about living the high life."

Ashley stomped back to her bedroom and pulled out the suitcase she'd been using for her life over the past several years. After throwing in several piles of clothes, she grabbed the coat she'd bought while in Wyoming the last time she'd left. This time, she wasn't willing to even look back, knowing she had to make a change in her life, and getting away from Quincy was the first step. She'd figure out what to do with the rest of her stuff later. There was no way she could spend another minute in this apartment.

Wheeling the suitcase down the hall, she grabbed her purse from the chair by the door.

"Where are you going? You can't just leave now." Quincy's

face was contorted with rage, the red making her look like an apple.

"Find someone else to be your maid of honor. I won't be back for the wedding." Shutting the door behind her, Ashley wanted to relish the triumph of leaving, but the tears welled, and she was sobbing by the time she'd made it to the small compact car she'd bought at the beginning of her travel business.

She drove the well-known roads to the airport and parked in the long-term parking. Before she packed up her entire life, she wanted to make sure she did everything she could to make something work with Preston, if he would forgive her for not knowing about the message.

It took a total of three minutes to book a flight from her phone, and she headed into the airport, determined to take this next step, more sure of it than anything she'd done before. After going through security and waiting at the gate, she pulled up the message she'd sent from Quincy's phone to her own. Was she too late? Would Preston still be interested in a relationship with her?

Opening up her Quickstagram account, she flipped through the photos she'd taken or had taken of her in all the exotic places she'd been, but even the close-ups showed a girl who wanted something more than this.

Going through her gallery of photos, she found one she'd taken of her and Preston that night after he'd rescued her, just before they'd kissed. Their smiles went from ear to ear, and there was something different in her eyes, like she'd finally found a safe space.

She just prayed it would all work out, that no matter how mad Preston was, he could forgive her for not telling him her feelings before she left for Mexico. She'd be by his side on the farm, every day mucking out stalls, if that's what it took to be with him.

CHAPTER 24

Preston wasn't feeling the festive holiday spirit at all. He'd seen the barrage of text messages Ashley had sent, as well as the few voicemails she'd left. But none of them mentioned anything about what he'd said in his message, and he didn't want to talk to her at all, just wanting to get back to the life he'd lived before he met her.

But was that even a possibility now? It seemed like she was everywhere he looked, whether in a memory together or in what he'd imagined for his future. He couldn't even milk the cows without seeing her next to him, helping.

"You sound like you're ready to battle the world today," Lauren said, walking up behind him.

"No, just trying to get the muck off this machine. Why can't anything stay clean in this place?" He took his rag and scrubbed more, doing nothing to what was now practically cement manure on the four-wheeler.

He'd begun cleaning different parts of the farm equipment and the stalls in between milkings, hoping it would take away his thoughts about Ashley. But the more he tried, the more she seemed to stick with him.

"I don't think I've ever seen this place so tidy. And when Mom was around, that's saying something." Lauren punched him lightly in the shoulder. "Why don't you at least answer her? She's made a serious effort to contact you."

Preston glared at his younger sister. "But she hasn't said anything about what I wrote in that message to her."

Lauren shook her head. "Now you sound like you're back in elementary school. Maybe she didn't see it. All you have to do is pick up the phone and say, 'Hey, I sent you this message, but in case you didn't get it, this is how I feel.' Easy peasy."

"It's not that easy." Preston ground his teeth together, feeling like his insides were going to burst into flames with the frustration coursing through him.

"It is. But you know what? I think you're scared. Scared that she'll say no. That she'll continue traveling the world without you. Or is it that you're scared she'll give up everything to be with you here at the farm?"

The truth of her words sank deep into his chest, making him wonder if it was easier to believe Ashley hadn't loved him in the first place so she wouldn't be giving up everything to be with him. He knew what it was like to give up the rodeo circuit to come home to the farm. He'd never be able to live with himself if she came to resent him the way he resented the cows he worked with every day.

"What are you doing here anyway?" Preston asked, hoping to avoid answering the question.

"I came by to bring Dad some caramels. I made some last night and thought he'd enjoy a few. I only came over here because I saw you scrubbing the side of this thing like you were hoping the color would come off."

Preston huffed. "I wasn't that intense."

Lauren's eyebrows raised, and she smirked. "Uh-huh. Just keep telling yourself that. I'm going to head in to see Dad. Let me know if you need to chat later."

Preston went back to cleaning the four-wheeler, making sure his movements weren't so intense. It was only a few moments later that he heard his sister's scream from inside, and he ran in, his blood pulsing in his ears.

He barely took the time to kick off his boots before running through the kitchen and into the living room where he found Lauren standing over their father, who looked to be unconscious on the ground.

"Call 911!" Lauren said, checking vitals and beginning CPR.

Preston pulled his phone from his pocket and dialed the three digits, trying to breathe as he waited for the line to connect. Shirley Blackburn, one of the dispatchers at the fire department, answered.

"Shirley, send an ambulance to the Burke farm. My dad's unconscious." He hung up and moved to kneel next to his dad and Lauren, his heart pounding in his throat. All the selfish thoughts he'd felt over the last few weeks paled in comparison to the thought of maybe losing his father. To be parentless at the age of twenty-nine wasn't something he'd imagined, but he hoped his dad would pull through whatever was happening this time.

"Does he have a pulse?" he asked his sister, hoping she'd have better news than what he was thinking.

She nodded. "It's faint, but there's something. Did they say how long until the ambulance gets here?"

"They were calling a few of the volunteers in, so probably a few minutes." Preston tried to think of something he could do, the panic starting to rise as he realized that if it took too long to get out to the farm, the chances of his dad surviving whatever condition this was would lower. He thought about loading his father in the car and driving him to the hospital, but he worried something would happen and he'd make things worse.

It seemed as though the seconds passed by like minutes, and everything slowed down to the point where he had to ask several times what Lauren had said.

"Get the door. I think they're here."

Preston shot up and made it to the door, letting the paramedics in. Through the whirlwind of it all, he watched as his father's color turned more ashen. Lauren came over and wrapped her arms around his middle, the two of them giving the paramedics room to work.

Once their dad was loaded into the ambulance, Preston and Lauren got in the truck and headed over to the small hospital behind the flashing lights, hoping they could do something to help their father.

When they made it there, the nurses informed them that it was a possibility that they would have to life flight him to the hospital in Idaho Falls, meaning it would be a longer drive to watch over him.

Lauren pulled out her phone to call Walker, and on instinct, Preston swiped to find Ashley's name. He wasn't sure what he would say, but he knew he needed to hear her voice, to hear her tell him that things would be okay, even if they wouldn't.

He waited impatiently as the dial tone rang over and over again, finally leading to the voicemail at the end.

"Hi, this is Ashley. I'm probably flying or at a beach somewhere. Leave a message, and I'll call you back when I can."

It was the same voicemail he'd heard a few times, but this time, just hearing that much made him relax a bit.

"Ashley, call me when you can. I know I've been a jerk, but I really need to talk to you right now." He did his best to disguise the emotion in his voice, the vulnerability rising up. "This is Preston, by the way. Call me."

He hung up and waited for Lauren to finish talking with the nurse.

"Let's go get the boys from school, and we'll drive to Idaho Falls. Walker and Easton will take turns milking until we can get back." Lauren's calm caused Preston to wonder how she still hadn't broken down in the midst of all the emotions in the last half-hour.

After checking out Seth and Tyler from the high school, they drove up through Thayne and started the journey over to the large town near the border of Wyoming and Idaho. Preston hated not knowing what was going on with his father, but they'd just have to hurry so they could get it all figured out.

$\mathcal{A}$shley rented a car at the Salt Lake International Airport, grateful for something that came with four-wheel drive as the snow started to fall. She'd booked it through there, knowing the drive to Coldwater Creek would only be a few hours, still getting her into the valley several hours before a connecting flight to Jackson would even take off.

She checked her messages and heard a plea from Preston to call her. Connecting the phone to the vehicle's Bluetooth, she dialed his number and took off driving.

It went straight to voicemail, making her wonder what could have happened to cause that much panic in him. Dialing Lauren's phone, she got the same thing, and a pit formed in her stomach, telling her something was really wrong. If both of them weren't answering, it had to be Mr. Burke.

She traveled on the freeway heading north, grateful that the snow hadn't started to gather on the roads just yet and was still melting on the warmer road. She just hoped she'd have the same luck all the way through. Racking her brain, she tried to think of some way to get information.

The phone number for the Afton hospital came up on Google, and she dialed it, not quite sure what she would say when someone answered.

"Afton Community Hospital, how many I direct your call?" came the voice of the operator.

"I need some information on a possible patient. Mr. David Burke."

After a pause, the woman said, "Let me transfer you to the nurses' station."

After a pause, another woman said, "Hello, this is Stacey. What can I do to help you?"

Ashley's mind was spinning faster than she could form words. "I'm a friend of the Burke family, and Preston called me a bit panicked but didn't say anything about the situation. I just wanted to rule out the fact that it might be his dad."

"So you're not a member of the Burke family?"

"No." The word was more bitter than anything she'd ever tasted.

"I'm sorry, ma'am, but I can't give out any information if you're not a direct member of the family." The woman's voice sounded apologetic, but Ashley's patience was running out.

"I'm driving from Salt Lake. Do I need to head to the Burke farm or somewhere else?" She gritted her teeth to keep from letting out an exasperated sigh.

After several moments of silence, the woman said, "Try the Idaho Falls hospital." The click of the phone told Ashley all she needed.

Pulling up the Maps app on her phone, she typed in the new destination, hoping she wouldn't miss anything on the drive.

She should have come days ago, rather than waiting to see what would happen. She just hoped Preston would forgive her for not being there from the beginning.

CHAPTER 26

The trip slowed down significantly as the roads were covered at this point by the heavy snowfall. Ashley made it to the hospital when the sky was dark and hurried into the emergency room, hoping to find someone familiar there.

She saw Lauren first, sitting in a chair next to the lobby area. Ashley ran over to her, her loud steps causing Lauren to look up in surprise.

"Ashley, what are you doing here?" Lauren stood, accepting the hug Ashley had for her.

"I got Preston's message and did a little finagling to get some information about where you might be. When you and Preston didn't answer, I called the Afton hospital, and the one nurse told me to head here."

Lauren sighed next to her. "I'm glad you're here. Preston has been a bear ever since you left for Mexico." She winked, and Ashley smiled, hoping her words meant Preston hadn't completely given up on her.

"How is your dad?" Ashley asked, sobering as she thought of the reason she was in the place that smelled of bleach.

"He's going to be okay, they think. They just brought him out of surgery, and Preston is in talking with him right now. He had a blood clot near his lungs, which made it hard to breathe, and he passed out. Do you want me to go get him?" Lauren motioned down the hall.

Ashley froze. Sure, she'd flown and driven for several hours to be there, but to actually face Preston now...she wasn't sure how to react to that.

She shook her head and took a seat next to Lauren. "No, I'm just here to help with whatever you need. Have you guys eaten in a while? Maybe I should run and grab some food."

Seth and another older boy with similar features to both Lauren and Preston turned the corner, small bags of candy in their hands.

"There's a cafeteria downstairs. Seth and Tyler just don't want to go down there." Lauren rolled her eyes, causing Ashley to laugh out loud.

Tyler smirked. "We survive on sugar every day at school and work. Why is now any different?" He grinned wide, and Seth chuckled beside him.

"Sounds about right." Ashley couldn't help but grin at the boys. She'd been an only child growing up, but it hadn't ever felt that way because she'd always had Quincy by her side. Now, though, seeing the boys joke around and Lauren's relationship with them, she wondered what that would be like, to have siblings who you trusted with your life and didn't have to question every move they made.

Movement down the hall caught Ashley's eye, and she turned, seeing Preston with his head down heading in their direction.

"Did you get a good lecture?" one of the boys asked, tossing a few pieces of candy into his mouth.

Preston's gaze rose and locked onto his brother. A sly but tired smile came before he teasingly punched the one who'd spoken. "No, no lectures this time. But Dad said he's waiting for you. I hope you get a good talking to."

The brother walked down the hall, his gait like that of most high schoolers.

Preston turned back to look at the other two, when his gaze caught on Ashley.

"Uh, how long have you been here? How did you even know we were here?" The suspicion in his face caused Ashley's heart to sink. Maybe it was a bad idea to just barge into what was a family situation because she wanted to tell the man standing before her that she loved him.

Lauren must have seen her face because she stood, grabbing her purse and Seth's arm, pulling him up from the chair where he had just sat down. "We're going to go see what they have left for dinner down at the cafeteria."

Ashley wasn't sure whether that was a good thing or a bad thing since her tongue was all tied in knots. After they disappeared down the hallway, she could feel Preston's eyes on her, waiting for a response to his question.

"Well, I, uh—I had some things I wanted to tell you, and when I got your message, I knew something was wrong. So I did my best investigative work and tried to get here as quickly as I could."

He shifted from one foot to the other, his posture still ramrod-straight. "So, you weren't just silencing my call earlier." The statement was a large knife to Ashley's chest, as though that one act showed her betrayal for the entire relationship.

Her irritation rose, feeling much like she had when she'd had to confront Quincy earlier that day. "I was already in the air, hoping to get to you as fast as I could because I love you and I didn't want to miss out on telling you that. But if you want to think that I'm some girl who can't be trusted to take a phone call, then maybe we shouldn't be together."

His jaw hung open, and his eyes searched her face, probably trying to decide if she was telling the truth or not.

Ashley folded her arms, not willing to back down from the challenge now.

When he didn't speak, she decided to go for the rest of it, hoping that all the pep talks and practice sessions she'd done on the trip here would be enough to ease her conscience, no matter what happened between her and Preston.

"I didn't have reception for the entire trip in Mexico, so Quincy was the one keeping up all the social media accounts. She found the message from you and deleted it before I could see it, all in the hopes that I wouldn't want to run back to you. She finally admitted it to me this morning, and I've been trying to get here ever since."

She wiped away a tear, wishing her emotions would stay strong for just a few minutes before she crumpled into a pile. "I don't know what I'll do or if I'll even continue to travel, but I wanted to see you, wanted to talk to you face to face so that if you don't feel the same, then I would know and could move on with my life." Taking a deep breath, Ashley rubbed the tip of her nose, hoping it wouldn't start running.

Preston took a step forward, and for the first time in almost a minute, Ashley looked up at him, seeing the hardness of his features had turned to something more tender and hopeful.

His hands reached out for her shoulders, and he ducked a bit to get a good look into her eyes. "Did you say you love me?"

Had she said that out loud? She'd been thinking it for the last one hundred and fifty miles, but she had told herself she wouldn't say anything until she knew how he felt.

"Maybe." She pinched her lips together, trying not to smile.

"So, you're done with Quincy and Jason?"

"Heavens, yes. I was thinking about starting a new venture but haven't quite figured out all the little ins and outs of it yet. Mostly, my thoughts were just about you and getting here. Worrying about this conversation for hours." Ashley glanced down, feeling more embarrassed that she couldn't control the run of the words tumbling out of her mouth.

He put his finger under her chin and gently tipped her head back. "Well, Ashley Morgan. I love you too. I think I have from that first time we hung out."

"But why didn't you say anything?"

With a mischievous smile, Preston said, "I didn't think it could ever work out. You had the wings to fly, and I was stuck in the same routine, day after day. I guess I was trying to convince myself that it wouldn't hurt as bad if I never admitted my feelings for you." He paused a moment, sliding his arms around her waist. "So you're willing to be the girl-friend and future wife of a dairy farmer?"

Ashley smiled wider than she had since she'd left Cold-water Creek. "Definitely."

"Well, I have to disappoint you, then."

"Wait, what?" She looked up at him, trying to guess what he was saying.

"I've just had a long talk with my father. Adam came to him a few days ago and said he'd be willing to take over the farm. He's put in a lot more time there lately, and I think he prefers being with the cows compared to people." His comment caused a deep, guttural laugh to escape from Ashley.

She nodded. "I'm sure that could be said about a lot of people. But what will you do? Go back to the rodeo?"

"No," he said, pulling her a bit closer. "I was thinking about doing some traveling with this girl I really like. She's got a lot of experience in that area, and I was hoping she'd be willing to show me around the world."

Left without words, Ashley rose up on her tiptoes and pressed her lips to his. They were warm and tingly, the electric shock much the same as their kiss that night next to the fire.

He pulled her closer, and she was left feeling that same safe warmth she'd been coming to love over the past several weeks.

Leaning back, she said, "I think she'd be up for that. As long as it involves more time spent with you, I couldn't think of a better way to spend life."

It was time for the Burke family Christmas party, held at the farmhouse the night before the actual holiday. Preston's father had come home from the hospital with strict instructions to rest, and Ashley had made sure she could take shifts to help out, knowing how busy the rest of the family was during this time of year.

Preston had flown with her back to Texas so they could clean out the apartment, making it their first road trip, and Ashley couldn't have asked for a better traveling partner.

Jason disappeared before the actual wedding, turning up in Las Vegas a few days after the ceremony was supposed to have taken place. Quincy started calling Ashley, telling her she needed money to pay for everything that didn't get covered. Because it was no longer Ashley who was getting married, many of the companies had charged full price for their services, something Quincy hadn't even considered. Ashley hired a lawyer once they got back to Wyoming and started the proceedings to sever the business between the two of them.

Her time with the Burke family since had been priceless.

She'd helped set up all the Christmas decorations and was even enjoying the layers of snow that had fallen in the previous week, something Preston kept saying would be around until next summer.

It had been difficult to figure out a gift for him that would convey how much he meant to her and still be something he would value, but as she wrapped it in the little box, she smiled, hoping he would like it.

She placed the box under the tree with several of the other gifts already there and moved into the kitchen to help Lauren with all the food they'd spent most of the day preparing. Lauren joked several times about how she hadn't been able to cook to save her life before she married Walker, but with his guidance, she'd come a long way. Ashley had to admit everything smelled really good.

"What can I help you with?" she asked Lauren, who was stirring something in a pot over the stove.

Lauren turned to her and grinned. "Why don't you go ahead and get ready? I think I've got just about everything ready for now. Once the milking and chores are all done, we'll be ready to get started."

"Are you sure? Because I was just planning to wear this," she said, looking down at the oversize sweater and yoga pants she'd been wearing all day. It had been nice to be comfortable while working in the kitchen.

Lauren turned to her, tapping her pointer finger to her lips. "When you moved everything here from Texas, didn't I see a glittery silver blouse? I think that one would be perfect for tonight. And a few curls in your hair would look so good."

Ashley frowned. "You want me to go back to the lodge and get ready-ready?"

"Why not? We still have a few hours until all the work is done so the guys can be mostly off tomorrow."

Confused, Ashley decided to take Lauren's advice, unsure if that was typical for their family gatherings. Maybe they all dressed up super fancy and if she came looking like that, she'd be embarrassed to be there.

Two hours later, she'd showered and curled her hair, also adding some light makeup to her features. She put on the blouse Lauren had described and decided to add a flowy white skirt and heels to go with it. She froze on the way out to her car and then from the car into the Burke farmhouse, but once inside, she couldn't tell a difference.

"I saw Walker's truck still at the lodge. Is he not coming?" Ashley asked, blowing on her hands as she walked into the kitchen of the farmhouse.

Lauren waved a hand in the air. "There's a family party he needed to finish setting up for, but he should be here before we get started." She paused and looked Ashley up and down. "You look amazing. Almost like a Christmas bride."

Ashley blushed. "That's funny. I've always wanted to be married around Christmas. It's such a magical time of year. Wait, why are you still wearing the same thing you were wearing when I left? Are you not changing?"

"Magical it definitely is." Lauren winked at her and moved away, not answering the question. What was she hiding?

The living room was empty except for Mr. Burke, and Ashley moved over to sit on the couch next to his recliner. "How are you feeling, David?"

"Very well, Ashley, dear. You look lovely. Have you made a Christmas wish?"

"A Christmas wish?" Ashley sat back.

The older man grinned at her. "It was something my wife started when we first had Preston. You concentrate on what you want most, and it will come true."

Ashley smiled a bit hesitantly, wondering if something

had happened to the people she'd already come to love in the last few weeks. "It sounds like you all think of Christmas as having some kind of special power to it."

"I think you'd be surprised. So, what is your Christmas wish?"

"I don't feel like I can really make a wish. All of mine have already come true this year." She racked her brain, trying to come up with something she would love to have, but all she could think of were the blessings of having an amazing boyfriend and family to be with at this time of year.

"Hey," Preston's voice came from behind her. She turned, and he kissed her forehead, leaving the smell of the outdoors clinging to her nose. "You look beautiful. I'm going to go change, and then I'll be back down."

"Ash, will you come give me a hand in here?" Lauren asked, calling from the kitchen. "I just need to get things out on the plates now."

As Ashley got closer, she saw the wide grin on Lauren's face. "Something is up, and I'm going to figure it out."

Lauren acted as though she were zipping her lips and turned to pull several trays of food from the large refrigerator, and Ashley busied herself with the food, plating it as though she were at a resort.

"Okay, I think we're all ready. Let's head out by the tree to get things started." It was only then that Ashley saw the change in Lauren's clothing to a form-fitting green dress.

The men of the family were joined by Walker, all dressed in suits.

Ashley looked around, searching for Preston's face in the small crowd. She felt his familiar hand take hers and turned to find him dressed in a blue suit and looking more handsome than ever.

His hand twitched a bit and then stilled.

"Are you okay?" she whispered, hoping to not embarrass him in front of his family.

"I have a gift I wanted to give you." He handed her a small white cardboard box. "Open it."

What could he have gotten her that she needed to open right now?

She lifted the lid off the box and gasped as she saw the small charm inside in the shape of a ring.

Preston sank to one knee, his eyes searching her face.

Ashley's heart soared, the feeling far surpassing the last proposal she'd been a part of.

"I had a hard time finding a charm that might symbolize something about your trip here. But when I saw that one, I just knew I wanted things to go a step further." He swallowed, tipping Ashley off to the level of his nerves. When he spoke again, his voice had more emotion to it, causing Ashley's eyes to water. "We've been through a lot in a short amount of time, but I want to be with you forever. Ashley Morgan, will you marry me?"

Pressing both hands over her mouth, she nodded, letting some of the tears escape. "Of course. Of course I'll marry you."

Relief passed over his face, and he stood, pushing a diamond ring onto her left ring finger. He bent in to kiss her, and she was sure her life couldn't get any better than this.

When he pulled back, Preston bit his bottom lip, looking as though he was deciding something else. He finally said, "I have one more surprise, but I want you to know that it's okay if you're not ready for it yet. I just remembered that you said you'd always wanted to get married around Christmas."

Looking around the room at all the family and friends she'd gained recently, she realized they were all a lot more dressed up than normal.

"Get married tonight?" She turned back to him with her eyes wide.

"If you want to, we are ready for it." He raised his hands, shaking just a bit once more. "I talked to your mom. She wasn't able to fly out to be here with you, but we could always video chat. But if you're not ready, if you want to wait and do more preparations, I want what you want."

She paused a moment, the tears welling up so much that it was difficult to focus in on his face. "You did all this for me?" Her voice came out little more than a few cracks in a whisper.

He shrugged. "I just wanted you to know it was an option."

"Let's do it. Now or later, I want to spend my life with you, Preston Burke."

* * *

Read Kassidy & Dustin's story in *Love in the Details.*

* * *

Thank you for reading *Love Locked!* If you enjoyed it, I would love to see a review from you. You can also subscribe to Britney's newsletter here:
Subscribe to Britney's List